SISTER FREVISSE MYSTERIES
BY MARGARET FRAZER

THE NOVICE'S TALE

Among the nuns of St. Frideswide were piety, peace, and a little vial—of poison . . .

"Frazer uses her extensive knowledge of the period to create an unusual plot . . . appealing characters and crisp writing."
—*Los Angeles Times*

THE SERVANT'S TALE

A troupe of actors at a nunnery are harbingers of merriment—or murder . . .

"Very authentic . . . The essence of a truly historical story is that the people should feel and believe according to their times. Margaret Frazer has accomplished this extraordinarily well."
—Anne Perry

THE OUTLAW'S TALE

Sister Frevisse meets a long-lost blood relative—but he may have blood on his hands . . .

Don't miss these compelling novels of medieval mystery—available from Jove Books!

THE
OUTLAW'S TALE

MARGARET FRAZER

JOVE BOOKS, NEW YORK

THE OUTLAW'S TALE

A Jove Book / published by arrangement with
the author

PRINTING HISTORY
Jove edition / February 1994

ISBN: 0-515-11335-2

A JOVE BOOK®
Jove Books are published by The Berkley Publishing Group,
200 Madison Avenue, New York, New York 10016.
JOVE and the "J" design
are trademarks belonging to Jove Publications, Inc.

PRINTED IN THE UNITED STATES OF AMERICA

10 9 8 7 6 5 4 3 2 1

O hateful harm, condicion of poverte!
With thurst, with coold, with hunger so confoundid!
To asken help thee shameth in thyn herte;
If thou noon aske, with nede artow so woundid
That verray nede unwrappeth al thy wounde hid!
Maugree thyn heed, thou most for indigence
Or stele, or begge, or borwe by despence!

"The Man of Law's Prologue"
Canterbury Tales
Geoffrey Chaucer

Chapter

1

THE GREEN SHADE of the forest was streaked and flecked with shifting gold sunlight. In the patterns of shadow and light, the dozen men sat or leaned or lay at ease against the great boles of the trees and their high-humped roots. Only their leader stood straight, his arms folded across his chest, his weathered, not unhandsome face creased deeply by his smile. "So," he said, "we're agreed we must not dine this day without an unexpected guest come to our table?" His men's grins answered his own at the jest.

Their leader eyed them all, considering, then said, "Will Scarlet, Little John—and, uh, Hal, Evan, you bring our guest from the greenwood road."

Will stood and swept his filthy red hat off in a bow that was far more elegant than his ragged-hemmed green tunic and patched-out brown hosen. "Master Robin, as you say, so shall it be."

But among the other men who had risen two were shoving at each other, trying to shoulder one another out of the way. "I'm Little John this time," the smaller of them claimed. "It was me he looked at."

The other, hardly medium-tall, made a rude noise. "Sit down, lack-inches. John was the big one. This is for me."

1

A third man lounged upright from a tree, broad-shouldered but no taller than either of them. "Now there you're both wrong. If anyone's Little John, it's me. And aside from the fact I can butt both your heads together when I want, I'm the best of us at quarter-staving."

"For which there won't be much use on this 'adventure,'" called one of the men still leaning against another tree. "Come on, Nicholas. Before it comes to blows. Which one is Little John?"

Their leader pointed at the medium-tall man. "You." And he added to the broad-shouldered man over the general laughter and comments, "You can go fetch the venison with Tom."

There was a groan from both Tom and the erstwhile Little John at that, and jeers at them from everyone else.

The chosen Little John went to join Will and Hal where they waited at the clearing's edge.

The fourth man, still stretched on his back with a root for a pillow, his eyes closed to the pleasure of a sunbeam on his face, said, "Maybe someone else instead of me. I might be recognized. She's not a fool, and neither is the steward."

Nicholas considered that and nodded. "Right enough. If this fails us, we'll need you for later. Cullum, go instead."

With a pleased chuckle, a short, freckled, brawny fellow rose to join Will and John and Hal. In a falsetto that went poorly with his wide chest he sang a cheerful parody of a maidservant's holiday song. "'I've waited long for today: Spindle, bobbin, and spool away! In joy and bliss I'm off to play, Upon the King's highway!'"

The four of them disappeared by a faint path into the leaf-shadowed forest, leaving more laughter behind them. Quietly, Evan said from where he still lay beneath the tree, "You know, Nicholas, you play that jest overmuch sometimes. I think there are days you really think you're bold Robin and we're his merry band."

*   *   *

The winter of the year of our Lord's grace 1434 had been cruel with frost and snow, and the spring had been harsh and cold. There had been fears of a famine year like last year, but May had come, and fair weather with it. Frevisse still wore the cloak she had put on at dawn when they left the priory, but now it was thrown back over her shoulders. Sister Emma had long since shed hers, with much fussing and bundling and wondering whatever could be done with it, until Master Naylor had taken it and strapped it with his own behind his saddle.

The three of them rode in no great haste, abreast across the crown of the road to avoid each other's dust. Frevisse had long since relaxed into the pleasure of the journey and the warm day, lulled by her horse's easy rhythm and soothed by the sweet air. She was even past being bothered by Sister Emma's chatter. Summer flowers arrayed the wayside grass and hedgerows with their rich yellows, purples, whites, and sometimes reds and sky-caught blues. Birds sang as if making up for their lost spring. Everywhere was green— fields and pastures and rough road edges well into their summer growth. Here along the uplands to where the road had climbed were flocks of sheep and their leggy, bright-faced lambs; the hollow clappering of their wooden bells kept company with the birdsong. The summer-smelling air was warm on Frevisse's face where it was free of her white wimple and black veil, and had found that after so long a confinement to nunnery walls, she had forgotten how wide the sky could be—deep blue today and adrift with mounded, shining clouds. And this afternoon they would ride through a forest. How long had it been since she had ridden through a wood?

They would be five days away from St. Frideswide's, Frevisse thought. Or more if the weather changed and they were delayed. She felt a little guilty at the pleasure in that thought, but reminded herself that she had come, not because she'd sought to, but as Domina Edith's choice for Sister Emma's companion.

But then, in all honesty, she suspected the prioress had chosen *her* to accompany Sister Emma to her niece's christening because Frevisse's winter restlessness had grown past hiding as spring came on.

The journey would have its trials. Sister Emma was a constant chatterbox whose tongue ran as if on wheels whenever freed from the nunnery's rule of silence.

But at the prioress's order to accompany her, Frevisse's winter longing had risen free in her like a fire blown upon, and Sister Emma's chatter had seemed nothing when set against the chance of riding out from St. Frideswide's into everything that had been calling to her all this while from beyond the priory walls.

Now, though, she had been in Sister Emma's company five unabated hours, and the pleasures of travel were already dimming under the constant flow of her voice and the knowledge that there would be four more days of it. They would reach Sister Emma's cousin's house before Vespers today, and tomorrow ride on in company with the family to her brother's house in Burford. The christening would be the day after that, and then two days to return to St. Frideswide's. She closed her eyes: five days of Sister Emma's unabated chatter.

"And it's so hot. I never thought it would be this hot. And it's only May. Still, that will help the hay along, I daresay, and that's to the good. Are the priory's meadows doing as well as they should be, Master Naylor? We nuns pay more attention to such things than you'd think, you know. And we notice when things go ill, and there's been enough of that lately, hasn't there? But it's all to the better now, I trust."

Master Roger Naylor, the priory steward, nodded. He had come with them as their necessary escort, and would ride on alone from Sister Emma's cousin's to tend to priory business in Oxford and return for them after the christening. He was not given to talk at the best of times, and his long, lined face rarely showed more than concentration on the task at hand. Frevisse suspected he had stopped actually heeding anything Sister Emma said miles ago.

"And the dust! Really, should the roads be this dusty so early in the summer? Are we short of rain? Hasn't it rained enough of late? I should think it had except this road is so dusty. And such heat. I could almost wish it were raining. It would be pleasant to ride in the rain, don't you think? A cool, gentle rain." She sighed at the blissful thought. "And I've read somewhere that rain is good for the complexion. Or maybe my sister told me that. Not my sister-in-law, who has the new baby—another girl, but they've had two boys too, so it isn't so bad—but my sister, Bertille. Yes, I'm sure she told me a gentle rain is good for the complexion. She always rinses her hair in rainwater and she's always had beautiful hair. It's a pity her nose is shiny pink. It's all those colds she has—not that I don't catch colds easily but not so easily as she does. You remember her, don't you, Dame Frevisse? She came to visit me Easter before last and brought me new handkerchiefs. I do go through handkerchiefs like a wastrel through his inheritance and was so grateful for them. But at least there's no danger of catching cold today, it's so hot!"

"It will be cooler in the woods," Frevisse offered.

"Yes, yes, it will. I do love the forest. I always have. All my family does. Oh, we did love to go Maying in the woods when I was a girl. Everything so beautiful . . ."

Frevisse did her best to stop listening.

The road dropped from the sheep-grazed uplands in long, easy slopes. There was a village, and they paused to buy ale and eat some of the food the kitchener had packed. Familiar, nunnery food of brown, unbuttered bread and some with-

ered apples from last autumn's harvest, tasting the better for
being eaten sitting on an unfamiliar well-curb. There were
few villagers about, everyone busy in the fields this time of
year. Only a threesome of small urchins in loose tunics,
barefooted and bareheaded, came to scuffle and stare at
them from a safe distance, and skittered off giggling when
Frevisse turned to stare back.

When they had finished eating, Frevisse found she could
have gone on sitting there a while in the pleasant sunshine.
It had been rather too long since she had been riding, and
there were already twinges of the stiffness she would have
tomorrow. Besides, the place was pleasant, the day was
hardly half gone, and they were already more than halfway
to Sister Emma's cousin's.

But Master Naylor rose and said, firm and sensible, "So
let's be on then."

"Neither fair weather nor daylight last forever," Sister
Emma agreed, "so journey while you may."

Sometime in her girlhood she had read a book of Wise
Sayings, and was fond of showing how many she remembered. Now she bounced to her feet and set about tidying her
black habit, brushing away crumbs real and imaginary and
straightening her wimple and veil. More slowly, Frevisse
followed suit, knowing what was coming. They had already
been through assisting Sister Emma onto her horse this
morning in the nunnery's stableyard; now the ordeal would
have to be gone through again.

At Sister Emma's fussy insistence, Master Naylor first
checked all her horse's girths and bridle straps to be sure
they were secure, and then that the horse was well tied and
could not sidle. She had chosen to have a box-saddle that let
her ride sitting sideways and lady-like; but since she was
somewhat short and round she could not mount it by herself
without an especially tall mounting block. St. Frideswide's
had had one, the village did not, and so Master Naylor was

going to have to take her by the waist and lift her into her saddle.

Frevisse expected Sister Emma would manage a lengthy session of false starts, reprimands, instructions, and fits of giggling at the impropriety of it all before letting Master Naylor accomplish his simple task. But Master Naylor grasped her firmly between his two hands, lifted her swiftly, and plopped her ungracefully into her seat before she had barely begun to squirm. Surprised and somewhat jarred, Sister Emma stared at him, words momentarily failing her.

Master Naylor turned away to Frevisse, who had been standing beside her own horse watching with unseemly amusement. She shook her head. A stableboy had held her bridle when she mounted this morning, but she was more confident now; old skills had come back to her. She had asked for an ordinary saddle, one that let her ride astride, the way she had ridden both in her childhood and after she had come into the care of her uncle Thomas Chaucer, who knew more than many about the manners of the best-born of England and agreed that safety and ease of riding were to be preferred over fashion. Now, with her reins gathered in her hand, she swung herself up into the saddle, ignoring Sister Emma's tut-tutting as completely as she had ignored it this morning. She smiled down at Master Naylor, and caught the trace of a smile at the corners of his mouth before he nodded to her and went away to his own horse.

The forest was not much further on. They approached it gladly and were thankful for its shade as they entered. Sister Emma exclaimed, "Such a blessing to be out of that dreadful sun. Oh, it's lovely here, so green and cool. Is the way short or long through here, Master Naylor? I hate to think we'll just be comfortable and have to go out again. Which way is it, Master Naylor?"

With an effort, the steward stirred himself to speak. "Which way is what, my lady?"

"Is this way long or short through the woods? I really don't want to be out in the sun again."

"There'll be woods until almost the end."

"Well, that's a blessing," Sister Emma said. "All the same, a dry May and a dripping June makes all things come into tune. Or so I remember it . . ."

Frevisse stopped listening again. There were the new savors of the forest to enjoy, and she did. By law the undergrowth was cleared well back on either side of the road, to leave no concealment for any one who might mean trouble. But the great trees had been left to throw shade across the road for travelers' comfort. The sunlight was gentled under the green branches, and the horses' hoof-falls and the creak of their harnesses were softened. Woodbine grew in the long grass of the verge, and though there was no bird song now in early afternoon, the flash of wings crossed their way now and again, and there were rustlings in the leaves.

They were somewhere several miles into the wood and had just crossed a stream when Master Naylor's head lifted a little higher with alertness and his hand went to his sword. "Other travelers."

"Oh, wonderful!" Sister Emma exclaimed. "We've seen nearly no one. Won't it be pleasant to see someone and wish them good day and God's blessing? A soft answer turns away wrath where a harsh word stirs up anger, so they say."

Frevisse sighed at this inapt quote and thought that they also said that a wise man conceals his wisdom while a fool announces his foolishness.

A bend and trees had hidden the other wayfarers until they were nearly met, but they were in sight now. Four men, all on foot, peasants by the look of them, bound for somewhere bearing bundles on their backs and trudging as if they had come miles already and had miles more to go. Probably sent by their lord on an errand that did not warrant better service, Frevisse thought. She was aware of Master Naylor eyeing them as he and she edged their horses sideways to give the men their share of the road. The men themselves also gave way, dropping into single file on their own side, their heads still down.

Sister Emma, never a steady hand on the reins and worse for her awkward seat, had fallen back as Frevisse drew aside, but could not manage her horse sideways out of the men's way. Frevisse turned in her saddle to frown at her as the first man passed her own horse. He would need to crowd to the roadside to avoid Sister Emma's.

But too suddenly for any warning, he dropped his bundle, straightened, and grabbed hold of Sister Emma's bridle. In almost the same moment, the other three men were in sharp motion with him, their bundles in the dust, one of them grabbing for Frevisse's reins, the other two leaping for Master Naylor. Frevisse jerked her horse's head away and tried to kick it forward, to ride the man down. But the horse was nunnery-bred, gentle to a fault; it balked and sidled and the man had her reins. Frevisse tried to kick at him but her skirts hampered her. He dodged without loosing his grip, grinning up at her.

Master Naylor, with two against him, was out of his saddle. One man had gripped his leg and heaved him sideways and over in a single motion, pitching him to the ground on the far side of his horse, while the fourth man ducked under the horse's upthrown neck to fall on him. Sister Emma, eyes shut and hands pressed to her cheeks, began to shriek, "Help, oh, Jesu, help, help, sweet Virgin, help, help!"

The man gripping Frevisse's bridle cried out as he grabbed her kicking foot, "Hold, sister, hold! We don't mean harm! Hold, for God's pity!"

He was ill-dressed and dirty, his red hat filthy, but his voice betrayed he was no peasant. Because of that, and because he wielded no weapon, Frevisse hesitated in her struggle. As she did, Sister Emma's shrieking ended abruptly, and Frevisse wrenched around to see her slumping limply from her saddle. The man beside her looked with panic from her to the horse, not certain if he should let go of it to catch her. Belatedly he tried to do both, but too late. Sister Emma slipped through his hold and fell to the ground with an untidy thump and lay still.

Frevisse's men seized her moment of distraction to let go of her horse, grab her instead by the skirts, and drag her from the saddle. Freed and at last frightened, the horse shied away, tossing its head to clear the reins from its feet. Frevisse, clutching at the man to keep from falling headlong, got her feet under her, shoved back, and tried to strike him. He caught her wrists. "Stand!" he ordered. "We have your steward and the other nun. Where can you run? Stand!"

Frevisse stood, braced against his grasp. Sister Emma was motionless in the road. Master Naylor lay face-down on the verge, his arm wrenched up across the small of his back toward his shoulders by a broad-muscled man straddling him at the hips. The fourth of their attackers stood over him, Master Naylor's sword in his hand.

"Yield," the man holding Naylor ordered. "We mean no harm to you or the sisters. Yield. There's no help for it."

His face white and screwed tight with pain, Naylor nodded. The man eased his hold, rose up from him, and stepped aside. Naylor, wincing, rolled over and sat up, nursing his arm for a moment before rising to his feet. His armed captor topped him by half a head, outmuscled him by several pounds, and was weaponed as well. But Naylor, facing him squarely, demanded, "What do you want? These are nuns, for God's sake. You're damned if you harm them, we've little to rob, and we'll hardly bring a ransom worth your while."

"We know who they are, and it's neither ransom nor robbery we want." The man was rougher of looks and manner than the one still holding Frevisse, but there was nothing threatening in his tone. He grinned. "All we ask is your company for dinner in the greenwood. Our master sent us for you."

Master Naylor's face showed his disbelief. "And I suppose your master's name is Robin Hood?"

The man grinned wider. "When it suits him. And that's Little John standing over yon fallen lady, not knowing what to do about her. And Will Scarlet is holding your other." He made a somewhat respectful bob of his head to Frevisse, then turned to the man beside him. "Hal, take his dagger too, and let's be away from here."

"Will someone come see to this one?"

The rather plaintive plea from the outlaw still holding Sister Emma's horse made Frevisse pull against her own captor's hold. "Let me go to her."

The man promptly released her with the sketch of a bow. She went to kneel beside Sister Emma, and found her breathing was suspiciously even and her color good. Somewhat more sharply than necessary Frevisse slapped her cheeks and said briskly, "Wake up, Sister. Wake up, or I needs must dash water in your face and spoil your wimple. You can't stay here. Wake up."

With soft groans and much fluttering of eyelashes, Sister Emma responded, looking first at Frevisse bending over her, and then at the man standing behind her. With a piteous moan, she turned her face away and shut her eyes again. "Oh, it's not a nightmare. We're ruined, Dame Frevisse. Ruined!"

With quelling asperity Frevisse said, "I doubt it." Whatever these men were about, it hardly seemed rapine or even robbery. But Hal had Master Naylor's dagger now, and the sword was still at the steward's chest, and none of them looked inclined to patience. The big man said, "We can't be biding here on the high road all the afternoon. Help her up and we'll be going."

Frevisse nodded and rose, pulling on Sister Emma's arm. Little John—and Frevisse doubted that was anything like his proper name—took Sister Emma's other one. Sister Emma shrank from him with small noises of distress and fear, but did not resist.

"Come on, then, Sister," the man said, not unkindly. "Let's be away from here." He grinned and added, "Welcome to Sherwood!"

Chapter

2

THE MAN CALLED Hal chose to be Master Naylor's keeper. He took the steward's sword belt to wear himself, notching it around his waist and sheathing the sword with a satisfied air. But he kept the dagger in hand at Naylor's back while two of the other outlaws tied the dropped bundles to the saddle of one of the horses, and Little John stayed guard by the women.

There being no help for any of it, Frevisse stood silently, while Sister Emma first pleaded to be set free, then threatened her brothers' vengeance on anyone who touched her, and the sheriff's full rigor if she wasn't sent on her way immediately, and finally—when no one paid heed to any of that—gave herself up to loud crying, clutching Frevisse for support.

Over Sister Emma's head, Frevisse met Master Naylor's questioning look and twitched her head in the smallest of negative gestures. There was no hope of any escape that included Sister Emma; she would be as burdensome as wet laundry. And as useful. Careful that none of the outlaws were looking at her, Frevisse silently mouthed, "You go." He had the best hope of escape, given any kind of a chance.

Grim-faced, Master Naylor shook his head. He was

bound by duty to protect them; he would not desert them, no matter how little help he could offer. And then the man who had captured Frevisse brought a rope from one of the bundles and, with Hal still keeping the dagger at his back, tied Master Naylor's arms behind him.

"Done, Cullum," he said.

They followed the road only a little way, then turned aside into a wide grassy path used by timber cutters, Frevisse guessed. But this was not the season for timber cutting, and the outlaws moved with an assurance that showed they expected to meet no one. Well away from the road, Will disappeared into the underbrush with the horses, one tied behind the other.

"Bring them back!" Sister Emma wailed. "You're stealing our horses!"

"They'll keep hidden till you need them again," said Cullum shortly. "You'll have them back. Now let's be away from here. Will can catch up."

"We're to walk? In the woods? Do you know what it's like in the woods? How can you expect me—"

Sister Emma's volume was increasing with every sentence. Reading the look on Cullum's face, Frevisse said hurriedly, "Hush, Sister. Be quiet! You're going to make them angry. You don't want them angry, do you?"

"My brothers will—" Sister Emma began loudly, then grasped what Frevisse was saying. She stopped, gaping, for a moment, then shut her mouth with an audible snap. Head hunched and hands clasped tightly under her chin, she began to pray. But inaudibly.

"Good," said Cullum. Beside him, Hal was tightening a blindfold over Master Naylor's eyes. Will came back, with a gesture to Cullum that all was well. Cullum nodded in reply and said, "Then let's be going. You'll be behind me, steward, with Hal to guide you. Then the women, with Will and John to see to them. No more noise than need be or we'll have to gag you and sling you from a pole and carry you like a deer's carcass. You understand?"

"Clearly," Master Naylor answered evenly.

Frevisse did not mistake his tone for submission. But Cullum, satisfied, said, "Good." He led them off the wide way for a narrower path deeper into the woods. Frevisse, hampered by skirts, wimple and veil among the branches and brush, was thankful she was at least unblindfolded and unbound. Dressed as they were, she and Sister Emma could not flee through the underbrush beyond the path, and the outlaws knew it.

And certainly Sister Emma had no thought of escape. She was too busy stumbling over everything in her path, untangling her veil from almost every branch, and sobbing under her breath every prayer she could remember, whether they suited their present trouble or not.

Ahead of her a branch slipped past Cullum's shoulder and whipped across Master Naylor's face. He flinched but made no outcry. Sister Emma stumbled yet again; John caught her elbow to steady her but she jerked it indignantly from his hold, then tripped again and fell to her knees with a miserable cry. Master Naylor started to turn, demanding, "What . . . ," but Frevisse said quickly, "It's all right. She only tripped," before Hal could do anything to him. He faced forward again, but Sister Emma wailed from the ground, "It's *not* all right! I can't *do* this!"

Before any of the men could intervene, Frevisse hissed, "Hush! They'll gag you if you keep on this way. Be quiet."

Sister Emma gulped, cast a cringing look at John looming beside her, and let Frevisse help her to her feet.

They went on. She pretended to be absorbed in managing herself and Sister Emma along the narrow path; but she was also trying to memorize the way they went—left along a dry stream cut, right at a fallen tree caught in the crotch of another, left again in sight of a tall broken stump. The way was deliberately tangled, she thought, and she was doubtful she would be able to find her way back even if she had the opportunity. But at least she could try.

At last they reached a large clearing. It was ringed by wide-trunked trees, with sunlight and flowers in its long grass and the air fragrant with the smell of roasting venison. A half-dozen roughly dressed men were scattered around in the shade. One of them, seated on a great tree root across the clearing, strummed lightly at a lute, so apparently at ease that he did not even look up as they came by. The others lunged to their feet, uncertain how to respond to the presence of two nuns in their midst. Except one, who moved forward with a confidence that said he was their leader.

He was perhaps near forty, dressed in the plain-cut green tunic of a forester, but the belt and pouch and dagger sheath at his waist were of richly finished leather. He was smiling, and there was charm in both his smile and the way he said to Cullum, "Take off his blindfold. There's no need now. Let him see for himself we mean no harm, neither to him nor these fair ladies."

While he spoke, he looked quickly, assessingly, from Sister Emma's rather dazed, damp, tear-reddened face to Frevisse standing cold-eyed and calm beside her. His smile deepened, and bypassing Master Naylor and Sister Emma both, he went down on one knee in front of Frevisse. "Good cousin, I pray your forgiveness for this unseemly meeting. I could find no better way."

Frevisse, ready for a great many possibilities at that moment but not that one, stared.

The man lifted his head. A little pleadingly, he said, "Don't you remember me at all then, cousin?"

Frevisse began to shake her head. But something in him—maybe the mischief behind his eyes even while he pleaded—awakened memory, and suddenly, despite the changes in him, he was familiar. "Nicholas!" she exclaimed.

Her father's older brother's elder son and indeed her cousin, though they had not met for almost twenty years.

He sprang to his feet, holding out his hands to her. "You'd always more wits than any three other women together. I knew you'd remember!"

In the surprise of the moment, Frevisse held out her own hands to clasp his. "Of course I remember! At Uncle Thomas's. You were there in his household that whole season from Michaelmas until after Christmastide." And had been sent away in disgrace, she remembered, because of too many jokes and insolences and finally for trying to seduce a serving girl.

There was clearly nothing of that scandal in Nicholas's mind. He grinned broadly at her, holding her hands in his own hard, strong ones. "You were an earnest creature then, forever tucked away in Uncle Thomas's library despite all Aunt Matilda tried to do to have you out of there. Are you still that earnest?"

"Are you still a teasing rogue?" Frevisse retorted.

Nicholas threw back his head and laughed. "Yes! Yes, indeed I am!"

"And you could find no other way for a reunion?" Master Naylor asked, his voice dry and edged.

Nicholas looked around at him with surprise, as if he had forgotten there was anyone there but himself and Frevisse. His demeanor changed quickly to apologetic. "Now here I'm at fault to neglect you, sir. And you, good lady." He turned his smile on Sister Emma, who in the surprises of the moment was staring from him to Frevisse and back again in a wonder both wordless and tearless. But as he bowed elegantly to her, she remembered herself and drew away from him with a sniff and a trembling chin.

Nicholas's smile turned rueful. "You've indeed been poorly handled, gentle lady. Let me make amends, I pray you." He stepped back, drew himself up straight, and swept a low bow to all three of them. "By your gracious leave, good master and fair ladies, let me invite you to our feast this day. We dine not elegantly but well, and I swear you would be no more honorably received in even the highest hall of the land."

Frevisse looked pointedly aside to Master Naylor's bound hands. Nicholas took her meaning and gestured to Cullum. "Free him. He knows now we mean no harm. I've given my oath and am Dame Frevisse's cousin into the bargain. He'll give no trouble. Will you, man?"

"Leave the ladies untouched and you'll have no trouble from me."

Nicholas put up a hand in ready oath. "As I pray for God's grace, they'll come to no harm that I can keep them from."

Master Naylor, rubbing his rope-marked wrists, eyed him coldly. Nicholas turned to Frevisse.

"There'll be food soon. Will you talk with me the while until we eat?"

Rather than answering, Frevisse was gazing past him at the lute player still strumming on the far side of the clearing. He had remained bent over his lute, his face half-unseen, but with an air of listening as intently as his fellows to everything that passed.

"I know him from somewhere," Frevisse murmured.

Nicholas glanced around to see whom she was looking at and shrugged. "I doubt it, unless your prioress lets wandering minstrels play for her nuns upon occasion."

Which Domina Edith certainly did not. But Frevisse was the priory's hosteler, in charge of the guests that the Benedictine Rule required every house to provide for. The lute player might well have spent the night some time.

The feeling was so strong that she would have gone to speak to him, but Nicholas led her aside to where a blanket had been spread at the foot of the largest tree. Sister Emma made to follow, but one of the outlaws stepped in her way. Tears threatened for a moment, but then Master Naylor took her by the arm, speaking quickly in her ear as he led her with the outlaw to another tree and blanket. Frevisse, satisfied they would be all right, gave her attention to Nicholas.

He gestured down. "Be seated, if it please you."

Grateful, Frevisse sank down on the blanket. It had been fine once, thick and closely woven, but was filthy now with hard use. Nicholas sat down on the tree root beside her and leaned forward, hands clasped between his knees. For a moment they looked at each other.

Frevisse remembered how he had been when they were young. He had been tall and still was, though somewhat stooped; he had been slender, he was now gaunt; his thick brown hair was further back from his forehead, and there was gray scattered through its curls. Laughter had always lurked behind his eyes, even in what should have been his most solemn moments, and it was still there. But so was weariness; and there were deep-set lines beside his mouth and around his eyes. He was older, and he had changed, except for the lurking merriment behind his eyes.

"You're looking more solemn than you need to, cousin," he said.

He had used to grin down at her much as he was doing now when about to tease away her anger at him. She was not angry with him now, nor much in the mood for being teased. "Remembering you and how you came to be an outlaw is enough to make me solemn."

"Ah." Nicholas looked away. "There were mistakes, and then more mistakes. Some folk—and particularly my father—always said I would go too far. One day I finally did. I've been paying for it a long time."

"Almost sixteen years."

"That long?" He looked a little startled, thinking of it, and then agreed. "Yes. It has been, I suppose. You always tended to be right. I remember that."

He had been in his early twenties, his father's heir to two good manors, when he ran afoul of a local lord unamused by some escapade of his. Frevisse did not know all the matter of it, but what had been a slight matter had escalated to a quarrel and then to an armed skirmish. Men had been killed on both sides, and Nicholas's own father had refused to back him or stand out against the decree of outlawry a Staffordshire sheriff had proclaimed. In answer, Nicholas had disappeared into the Derby hills, and that had been the last Frevisse knew of him until today. The Derby hills were a long way from southern Oxfordshire.

"Your father died," she said.

"I know. I—used to learn things. About home. But it's been a while now. Edward?"

"He was well, the last I heard, a year ago. And his wife and children."

"He has children?"

"Two sons and two daughters. The oldest boy is named Edward after his father."

"And the younger? Not Nicholas by any chance?"

"Not by any chance," Frevisse agreed. "He's named after his grandfather."

Nicholas looked down at his hands. They had been clever, graceful hands when he was young. Now they were broad and blunt, roughened and weather-browned like his face. Barely above a whisper he said, "I want to return home, cousin. I repent my sins, all of them. I want the king's pardon so I can return home."

Frevisse said nothing, not knowing what to say. Nicholas gripped his hands together tightly enough the knuckles whitened. He looked at her with tears in his eyes, and his voice was edged by a quiver he could not control. "It's been sixteen years. Long years. I want a pardon and an end to this."

Frevisse hesitated, then said, "Is that why we're here? Why I'm here? Because you want a pardon and you think I can win one for you?"

"You were Thomas Chaucer's pet when you were in his household, and word runs that he's still fond of you. He even comes to see you in your nunnery and takes an interest in its business because you're there."

"Yes." How Nicholas knew that she did not know, but she could guess how pleased he had been to learn it.

"If you asked him—told him I'd truly changed and were truly repentant—if you begged him in my name for a royal pardon for me and my men, he could get it. It would be easy for him, wouldn't it? Knowing whom he knows. High in the government as he is. He could do it without thinking twice, and he would if you asked him."

"He might but . . ."

Frevisse thought there were reasons it would not be as simple as Nicholas wanted it to be, but before she could gather them, Nicholas leaned forward to clasp her hands. She let him, but kept her own hands passive, her expression unresponding as he went on earnestly. "He would, cousin. For you he'd do it. Gladly do it. It would be such a very little thing for him to manage. Hardly a ripple among his great affairs of state. But it would be life to me. And to my men."

Frevisse looked around the glade. "You and your men seem to be living well enough, Nicholas. Free and well-fed and reasonably prosperous by the look of it. I've seen honest peasants living worse."

She was not purposely goading him, only talking while she tried to understand the possibilities and probabilities of what he was asking. But he let go of her hands abruptly and stood up, saying sharply, "Not so prosperous. Tired old clothes and chance-got food and never any certainty whether we can sleep in the same place two nights running or if this is the day we meet someone willing to shoot us dead."

Frevisse was aware that every other movement and voice in the glade had stopped. Despite his passion Nicholas had kept his voice low; no one but herself had heard him. But his sudden movement, his intensity, told enough. Everyone was looking. And for just a moment, as Nicholas realized that he had made his best argument and she was not readily agreeing, Frevisse saw his uncertainty.

Then from across the glade the lute player struck a long chord, breaking the moment with cheerful ease, and stood up. "If that venison isn't done by now," he said loudly, "I vote we eat it raw. Who's with me?"

Chapter

🔶 3 🔶

THEY DID NOT feast in the great glade, but were led a little ways away to a smaller clearing set up for cooking and sleeping. Logs, some of them crudely smoothed for easier sitting, had been put around a firepit where the venison—cut into chunks and spitted on skewers over the flames—was roasting. With ceremony more grand than the setting, Nicholas seated Frevisse, Sister Emma, and Master Naylor on logs comfortably away from the fire's heat.

"And I shall serve you myself, on bended knee," he said with a laugh. "Evan, a livelier air to suit this glad occasion."

The lute player, somewhere behind them, obliged. He was not particularly good, but at least did not stop after every wrong note.

True to his word, Nicholas waited on them, with all the manners he had ever learned in his father's and Thomas Chaucer's households, even down to the towel laid over his arm as he brought them their meal. His elegance contrasted with his rough forester's clothing, the somewhat grubby towel, and the meal of fire-blackened venison served in wooden bowls with a chunk of day-old bread on the side and ale drawn from a barrel set up and bunged on a stump across the clearing. But the meat was succulent, and

Nicholas—as aware of the contrast as Frevisse was—made his serving into an amusement of manners, so that Sister Emma, at first sitting very straight with determined indignation and her eyes still pink from weeping, forgot herself and laughed at something he whispered in her ear as he bent to pour more ale in her wooden mug. By the time the dishes were gathered up and carried away for cleaning, she had forgotten herself so far as to beckon him down so she could whisper something in his ear that made them both laugh.

Frevisse, meeting Master Naylor's silent look over Sister Emma's shoulder, knew he was neither charmed nor off his guard, any more than she was. There was a bramble scrape along his chin and the red welt left by a tree branch on his cheek, and Frevisse thought he moved as if his right side pained him, perhaps from the fall from his horse.

When the meal was done, Nicholas led her away from the others again to sit beside him on a log on the other side of the firepit.

Evening was drawing in by then. At St. Frideswide's the nuns would be gathering for Compline prayers on their way to bed. Here, someone added wood to the fire now that the cooking was done. The flames lapped up jewel-bright in the deepening twilight. Some fat caught in the new heat sizzled and a green log cracked loudly open, sending sparks upward with the smoke.

"I trust," said Frevisse, "that was red deer we were eating."

Under forest law, the red deer was the only kind that could be freely hunted. Too protective of its territory, the red bucks drove roe and all other kinds of deer away, reducing the sport for the nobility.

Hand on his heart to prove his sincerity, Nicholas replied, "Would I presume to give you anything else?"

"Yes."

He grinned at her the way he always had when his teasing

made her curt. It was surprising how many memories she had of him from that brief time they had been acquainted in Chaucer's household. He had been intelligent, charming— especially when in another scrape—and all around a slippery-tongued boy, as now he was a slippery-tongued man. "I remember that smile boded ill," she said.

He laughed outright. "I remember too. It barely worked better on you than on Uncle Thomas. He'd fix on me with those eyes of his and I'd know he was judging how many layers of flesh he'd have to flay away before he reached the bone."

Frevisse opened her mouth to answer but Nicholas forestalled her, leaning toward her and taking earnestly hold of her hands. "Cousin, cousin, I'm sorry for who I was and what I am. Believe that."

He was watching her face and must have read her doubt more plainly than she wished. He tightened his hold on her hands and said more desperately, "A man can change. Truly he can. Remember . . ." He cast around for an example. ". . . St. Anthony. After a misspent youth, his heart changed and he became a saint."

"You're planning to become a saint, Nicholas?"

His laugh was rueful. "No hope for that, cousin. I simply want to be a man with a home, a settled place where I don't have to be forever on my guard." His grin faded. Quietly he said, "It was a cruel winter, cousin, and my bones are none so young anymore."

There was a depth of feeling and pain behind his words that Frevisse, with memories of the past winter and pains of her own and knowledge of time slipping away around them every moment of their living, responded to.

But even as she thought it, Nicholas leaned toward her, lowering his voice to show this was between only the two of them.

"Truly, cousin, I've kept within the law these three

years." Frevisse raised her eyebrows at him. He looked away, shaking his head. "No, you can't believe that but it's true."

"Until today," she said.

"Until today, yes. But that was only because there was no choice. I couldn't come into your priory, could I? Couldn't ask for what the law forbids anyone to give me—shelter, food, even a cup of water on a hot day—and ask you to talk with me there where I was any man's prey."

"You're very unlikely to be recognized."

Nicholas shook his head again, a little more desperately. "I haven't stayed alive this long by letting myself be seen. I couldn't think of any other way to safely talk with you. Listen, I know I can't keep you here long. I don't mean to, believe me. So have you thought about what I asked? Will you do it?"

Frevisse wanted to know more than what she did, and said instead of answering him directly, "You want me to ask Thomas Chaucer for a royal pardon for you."

"And for my men."

"I don't know about the other outlaws, but a pardon will do you little good. When you were put outside the law, you lost claim to everything you would have inherited. It all went to Edward as surely and irrevocably as if you had died. That will not change. You'll be a landless freeman, nothing more."

"But Edward had a soft heart," Nicholas said. "And Father's holdings were ample enough. There's surely some corner for me."

"You're willing to live on Edward's charity?"

"On my brother's love and forgiveness."

"If he gives you anything at all. He does not have to. And he has four children now to provide for. I doubt his heart is more soft to you than to them."

"That I'll worry over when the time comes. It's my freedom from outlawry I want, and let God see to the rest.

Isn't the grace to be merciful among the things you pray for in your nunnery?"

To that Frevisse had no answer except, after a moment's silence, "I'll write as you ask."

Relief surged over his face. He squeezed her hands with fierce gladness, kissed her soundly on the cheek, and exclaimed for everyone to hear, "You are a pearl among women and a joy to my heart. We'll settle all tomorrow. Now let me see to my other guests because I've been a most neglectful host this while and while!"

Before she could stop him, he kissed her other cheek and strode gaily off toward where Sister Emma and Master Naylor still sat among his men.

Frevisse stayed where she was. She had things she wanted to ask him, especially about when and how he meant to free them now that he had her word. But she judged she should best wait for a less obvious time. Nicholas was rarely biddable when pushed, she recalled.

Frevisse rose from her log. She wanted to speak to Master Naylor and now was the most likely time for it. But before she reached him, threading her way among the outlaws, Cullum shifted from among them and, maybe to be more near the fire, went to sit on Naylor's other side where she had meant to. Trying to look as if it did not matter, Frevisse sat somewhere else and waited for another chance.

In the last of the daylight one of the outlaws was juggling three stones and making a joke of dropping one now and again on his toes. Sister Emma giggled every time he did, and so, for the climax of his act, he dropped one on his head, to the general merriment of his fellows. Frevisse, clapping with the rest as he took his bow, thought with a corner of her mind that he rubbed his head with more than pretended pain, and wondered why hurt was supposed to be funny.

Chapter

4

WHEN FREVISSE AWOKE, her first thought, even before she opened her eyes, was that it was raining.

Her second thought was that she was getting wet.

Not very wet yet, but the casual cover of leafy branches tied over the rough lean-to frame was not holding back all the steady patter of rain, and would probably hold back less as it continued.

Frevisse opened her eyes and sighed, resigned. She knew the open life of forest and road was not spent all in shady glades under warm skies. This morning what there should have been of dawn was gray half-light, and besides the gentle rattling of rain among the trees, there was a dripping near her ankle from a gap in the leafy roof. She sat up and reached for her carefully folded veil under the wad of sacking that had been her pillow. For decency's sake she had worn her wimple through the night as well as the rest of her clothing. Now she straightened it and by touch—familiar from years of rising in the night to prayers at Matins and Lauds—pinned the veil in place over it.

Sister Emma still slept in a scrunched huddle at the back of their small shelter. After she had stopped exclaiming happily about how really this was such an adventure and so exciting and weren't these folk surprisingly nice—considering they were outlaws, and was Nicholas truly her cousin? Amazing!—she had fallen to soft, irregular snoring, with her knees in the small of Frevisse's back for most of the night. For that, and for her unconsidering delight in Nicholas's company, Frevisse was in no charitable mood toward her now. But she was careful not to wake her. Frevisse harbored no doubts about Sister Emma's reaction to spending the day in rainy woods.

Others were stirring among the rough shelters of the outlaws' camp. Taking her blanket with her, Frevisse crawled out of her own inadequate shelter. Someone had stretched a canvas on poles over the firepit; a tendril of dispirited smoke was rising under it, nursed by the lute player.

Frevisse picked her way over the mud toward the fire, her blanket wrapped around her shoulders. The lute player had kindling-cut a log, and was feeding the dry splinters from its heart into a tiny nest of coals among the damp logs. The splinters were beginning to flare in tiny flames and the logs to steam in the growing heat. In a while, with patience, he would have a decent fire despite the weather.

As she sat down on her heels, her skirts bundled under her, the man glanced at her and said, "Good morrow, my lady. Though it isn't very good, is it?"

"At least you've saved the fire."

"Small pleasures can be life's greatest, I was told as a lad. I think the ordinary pleasure of fire will be very great this dour morning."

As faces went, his was not a handsome one. Something seemed to have gone wrong in its making: cheek, forehead, chin seemed not quite meant for the same person. But his eyes were deeply brown, and smiled when his mouth smiled, with a warmth and intelligence that made handsome or unhandsome rather unimportant.

And now Frevisse recalled him.

A week before he had stayed overnight at the priory guesthouse; he had been a peddler, had chatted and jested with the priory servants, and done a satisfactory bit of selling among them. As St. Frideswide's hosteler, Frevisse had noticed him. "You seem to have lost your pack somewhere."

He smiled at her over the fire. "I was afraid you'd remember me."

"But hoped I wouldn't?"

"Hoped, but expected you would."

"You could have stayed away while I was here."

He shook his head. "The plan is as much mine as Nicholas's. I had to be here."

"*You* told Nicholas I'd be coming this way."

"I went to St. Frideswide's to find if there were a way he could safely contact you. When I heard you were going to be outside the nunnery, this seemed our best chance, yes."

"You were called Evan then."

"And I still am."

The fire had strengthened enough now that he laid on the rest of his kindling and began to make a tent of larger sticks over and around it. One of the men whose name Frevisse had not yet heard came over with an iron tripod and stew pot. "You watch this?" he asked, and Evan nodded. The man stuck the tripod legs into the soft earth around the firepit and hung the pot over the growing blaze, then walked off.

"Stew," Evan said. "From last night's venison. Warm food will help this day. The rain looks like it's going on."

Frevisse was less interested in the stew than in him. "So you're more outlaw than peddler?"

Evan shrugged. "I'm this and that. Six of one and half a dozen of the other. Though I can't recall any particular law I've broken of late."

"But you're in need of pardon with the rest?"

"Aren't we all in need of pardon, my lady? For some of us, God's forgiveness will be sufficient. For others"—he gestured around the clearing—"more earthly ones are necessary."

"Especially if you kidnap nuns," she said tartly. The way his words slipped out from under what she wanted to know reminded her of Nicholas.

"Especially then," he agreed. "But there's no harm meant to you or your companions. And we are in need."

He had been plausible as a peddler, clever at his patter and flattering to the servant women. He was plausible now, without the patter or the flattering, and less like an outlaw than the others.

She said, "You'd better find a way to stir that stew if you don't want the venison more burned than it was last night."

He stood up and went away. Frevisse, holding out her hands to the fire's growing warmth, became aware of whimpering from the lean-to behind her and sighed. Sister Emma was awake. The whimpering coalesced into definite complaining, and Sister Emma with her veil askew, her blanket huddled around her shoulders and clutched over her chest, came scurrying through the increasing rain to the fire.

"Oh, Dame Frevisse, what's happened to the day? This isn't what I expected at all!" Huddling and shivering, she crowded to the flames near enough to scorch her skirts. "What are we to do?"

Frevisse rose and drew her a pace back from the fire. "Our morning prayers, I think. We rather shorted Compline last night." In fact they had whispered hurriedly through a brief version of the service as they settled to sleep; and Frevisse had not awakened in the night for Matins and Lauds at all.

"Oh, yes. Of course. But it's so strange to be saying Prime here, isn't it? And everything is so wet. Not right at all. A place for everything and everything in its place, and this just doesn't seem the place."

"Everywhere is the place for prayers," Frevisse said.

"I know that," Sister Emma said with a trace of peevishness, and sneezed. She bowed her head.

While they went through as much of Prime as was required of them while on a journey, Evan returned with a wooden spoon to stir the stew. Its savoury odor troubled Frevisse's concentration, and apparently Sister Emma's too, because directly on the end of the last amen, she exclaimed, "That smells *so* good!"

"Last night's venison with wild onions and some few other herbs to hand in forest and field," Evan said. "But somewhat short on salt, I fear." He called across the clearing to someone, "Ned, bowls and spoons. This is ready, I think."

"How far did you have to go for that deer?" Frevisse asked. "Even if it is red deer, which I doubt, you surely didn't kill it near here."

"And why not?" asked Evan with a glint of amusement.

"Because let any forester find evidence a deer has been taken and he and his men will scour for miles to find the man who took it."

"You're very knowledgeable for someone who lives behind nunnery walls."

"I didn't always live behind nunnery walls. How far did you go?"

"Far enough that no one will think to look here for their carcass."

And now Ned came with bowls and spoons for them, and the other outlaws were gathering into the scant shelter of the canvas with oddments of bowls and spoons of their own. Nicholas appeared. He had taken time to smooth his clothing, but his jaw was shadowed by beard and his hair only roughly combed; warm food came before most other things on a day like this. To Frevisse's relief, Master Naylor was behind him. Still guarded by Cullum, he was rubbing his right wrist. Frevisse saw red marks around both it and his left one, showing he had been tied through the night.

Forgoing any greeting, she said sharply to Nicholas, "You tied him like a dog! There was no need for that!"

"Lacking your kinship to me and Sister Emma's kind heart, Master Naylor is not fond of me or the matter between us at all," Nicholas said calmly. "He might balk at killing me in my sleep, but not at escaping if he had the chance."

"I've agreed to deal with Uncle over your pardon. Master Naylor isn't going to bother with escape when you'll be letting us go this morning anyway."

Evan put a warm bowl of stew into her hands. She took it without looking away from Nicholas, who showed slight embarrassment and some amusement. "Cousin of my heart, I can't let you go so soon. You haven't written the letter and I haven't Chaucer's promise back."

"Nicholas! You cannot keep us until you have an answer! We were expected somewhere last night and there'll be trouble when we don't come today. And who knows where Uncle may be? He has manors all over southern England. He could be anywhere. Even in London. It's going to take time for a messenger to find him."

"He's at Ewelme," Evan said, handing a bowl to Sister Emma.

"Peddler's knowledge?" Frevisse demanded.

Evan smiled his smile. "When one knows how to ask—or who to listen to—one can learn all manner of things."

Frevisse turned back to Nicholas. Ewelme was in reasonable reach, a solid day's riding away, but that did not solve other problems. "We're expected at Sister Emma's cousin's early today at the very latest."

Sister Emma swallowed stew and sniffed moistly. "And

at my brother's tonight. There'll be no end of trouble if we're not there."

"Naylor will take a message from you to your cousin or your brother or whoever best needs it," Nicholas said. "We don't want trouble stirred up that way. He can be on his way when he's finished eating and that will be one problem settled."

Master Naylor straightened. "I'm not taking a message anywhere nor leaving these women here alone. They were put in my charge and in my charge they stay. When I go, they go."

Anger tightened Nicholas's face. "They're in *my* charge now. You'll do what you're told."

"I want to go," Sister Emma fretted. "I could be warm there, and dry. I feel a chill, I really do. I do need to be warm and dry or I'll catch one of my dreadful rheums. I know I will." She sneezed as if to prove it.

The men ignored her. "I'm not leaving them," Master Naylor said.

"You will if I say so," Nicholas answered.

Master Naylor shook his head, face stubborn-set. Nicholas closed on him with a rising fist, but Evan caught his arm with seeming casualness and said, "I think it's for Dame Frevisse to persuade him, Nicholas. He'll take her word long before he takes your blows. And you're frightening Sister Emma."

Sister Emma had begun to pat at her gown and peer up her sleeves. "My handkerchief. Where is it? It's white linen, very nice, with leaves embroidered on it. Green leaves. I really do need to wipe my nose."

Frevisse, annoyed, said, "Here's mine," and handed her a plain one, then laid a hand on Nicholas's other arm as she said to Master Naylor, "We'll be well enough here. We'll be well taken care of, I'm sure." She kept her voice even, but her gaze was intent on Master Naylor's, willing him to listen. She had never known him to give way to temper, but she suspected he had one, and that he was now near to losing it. "Nicholas is seeking a pardon and won't endanger that or his soul by allowing us come to any harm. He probably has the right of it that we'll all be well if you go to quiet any fears there maybe growing. We'll come to no harm in his keeping. Truly."

"I'm getting *wet*," Sister Emma complained. The outlaws around the stewpot—more interested in breakfast than in arguing—had jostled her halfway out into the rain. She shook her damp skirts and crowded up against Frevisse's elbow. "Is it ever going to stop?"

No one answered her. Master Naylor and Nicholas stared at each other past Evan and Frevisse, until Frevisse said as persuasively as she might, "Please, Master Naylor. Sister Emma and I are in no danger here." She wanted to add, *But you are*. Nicholas had never been able to endure authority, and Master Naylor was not about to give his up. Keeping her tone mild, she said, "It's better you go ease the minds of those worrying over us. Nicholas and I will work out what needs to be said to Master Chaucer, and then surely he'll give us escort back to St. Frideswide's."

"Will he?" Master Naylor said with an edge of scorn, his stare not wavering from Nicholas's own glare. "Which of his men's necks will he risk on that venture on the open road, do you think?"

"We'll manage something," Frevisse said. Once the warning was out, it would indeed be less safe than ever for Nicholas or any of the outlaws to show themselves. "We'll manage by my staying with you. Or your coming with me. Those are the only choices."

"I make the choices here," Nicholas snarled. "And I give the orders."

"Not to me, you don't!" Master Naylor snapped back.

Nicholas jerked loose of Evan's hold to smash his fist at

the steward's face. Faster than Frevisse could follow, Naylor's left arm came up to block the blow while his right fist drove up under Nicholas's chin. Nicholas staggered, lost his balance, and fell in the mud beyond the firepit.

Shock held everyone motionless the length of an indrawn breath. Then Nicholas, scrambling to his feet, started for Naylor in unleashed fury. Frevisse moved to come between them but Evan was faster. He threw himself against Nicholas, pinning his arms while shouting "Hold!" in a roar that stopped both Nicholas and the other outlaws, who had begun coming to his aid.

"Now, listen," Evan said in the brief advantage of silence then, directing his words at Master Naylor but meaning them for everyone. "The choice is neither yours nor Nicholas's. The choice lies with the ladies. They surely want people to know they are well so no hunt will be set up for them. That could be dangerous for us and therefore for them too. They also must know that we'll arrange for their safe return to the priory. It can be done. We only need to think on it. But not now." He looked at Sister Emma. "You're willing to miss the christening?"

"Oh, yes." Nicholas had clearly persuaded her of his penitence last night; she was definite. "The pardon is far more important than a christening. It's Nicholas's life in peril, you see."

"The christening is to guard a soul," Master Naylor pointed out.

Considering two sides of a problem at once was not among Sister Emma's talents. Her face puckered with the beginning of thought. Frevisse interposed, "Someone else can stand godmother to the child, but no one else can see to Nicholas's pardon."

"And if Sister Emma is willing to stay, and so is Dame Frevisse," Evan quickly said, "and they're both willing for you to go"—Nicholas, still glaring at Master Naylor, pulled against Evan's hold but Evan's grip did not slacken—"then there are no grounds for your staying, not when you're needed elsewhere to reassure people of their safety."

Master Naylor looked straitly back at him, as if nothing this side of the word of God would shift his opinion. "Sister Emma, you can't want to be left here like this," he said. Sister Emma looked from Evan to the steward to Nicholas, who—finally grasping what Evan was about—had relaxed in his hold and smiled at her. The faintest lift of the sad corners of his mouth and his eyes said he would understand and forgive if she failed him now.

Sister Emma with final resolve and a wipe at her nose said, "I can't go. I really can't. Dame Frevisse can't be left here alone, and Nicholas needs her for his pardon. And you really should let my family and Domina Edith know we're safe."

Master Naylor turned to Frevisse. "Dame Frevisse—"

But Nicholas, shaking off Evan's loosened hold, said briskly, "That's settled then, so you'd best be on your way. Cullum, Will, Ned, see Naylor to his horse and the highway."

Chapter

🦋 5 🦋

THERE WAS NOWHERE comfortable to sit, and almost nowhere dry. Sister Emma made shift to sit on a log dragged near to the fire for her convenience. Still clutching her blanket around her shoulders, she began eating one-handed, her bowl balanced precariously on her knees. With a deep sigh, she regretted that she had no ale. Nicholas, just taking his own bowl from Evan, sketched her a gallant bow.

"My pleasure, lady, to serve you. Let me bring you some," he said, and went away with his own full bowl and a nod of his head to Frevisse.

Frevisse was too relieved to have Master Naylor safely away to want to push Nicholas now. She let him go and, preferring to stand rather than find a damp seat, set to eating her own stew before it cooled more than it already had. She fully meant to talk to Nicholas about his intent that she stay until all was settled, but warmth and food first, to face the day a little better.

She ate quickly, and then huddled her blanket up to her ears under her veil and around her shoulders and went to walk some warmth into her bones. If she kept under the edges of the trees, she could stay almost dry and keep the chill at bay.

She was watched, she knew, but no one stopped her, and she did not try to leave the clearing, though she suspected there were other clearings close by and that Nicholas had probably gone to one of them. Let him come when he would; he would have to seek her out sooner or later and she found she was willing to wait. In fact, she found she needed to bite the inside of her lower lip to keep a smile from her face as she walked. All the encrustation of little rules from the nunnery were dropping away here in the forest. For just today she had no duties, no one to answer to, no one to heed what she did. Under the overcast, she could not even tell the time of day for prayers, for her the best part of the great Rule she lived under. In place of them, she could at least have solemn thoughts on the trouble she was in; but she found instead that a child-simple tune and its words were running unquenchably through her head. "Rain before seven, done by eleven. Rain before seven, done by eleven. Rain before . . ." And a memory of dancing down a muddy road with her irrepressible parents one warm and rainy spring day in—France? Probably France. She had been very small and it had not mattered where they were. Her parents, holding her by either hand, had lifted her off her feet at every repetition of "seven" and "eleven," all three of them laughing at the rain and for pleasure of the road and traveling together.

The memory was too clear; she realized she was humming aloud as she walked and that nearly her feet were starting the skip and run that went with the words.

Startled, she subdued both urges. A tendency for her thoughts to wander had been one of her weaknesses in her first nunnery days. She had used the psalms as discipline: whenever she had caught her mind beginning its wandering, she had turned it instead to any of the many psalms she had memorized, to shelter her from her own lack of concentration. Now, firmly, and seemingly at random, her mind went to Psalm 148, finding the Latin first—*Laudate Dominum de coelis*—but shifting without intention to the English of her uncle's Wyclif Bible. " 'Praise the Lord you beasts and useful beasts, praise him you blooming trees and you cedars. Praise him you storms and floods—' " *And you drizzling days and damp,* her mind irreverently interjected so that she nearly laughed out loud. She was happy. Simply, unreasonably, unsuitably happy.

"Dame Frevisse, I'm *wet!*" Sister Emma's complaint penetrated the dripping breadth of the clearing. "Can't you *do* something?"

Jarred back to other people's realities, Frevisse sighed and crossed to the shelter over the fire.

"I'm wet," Sister Emma repeated, deeply aggrieved. "And I can't seem to warm."

"If you walk, you'll be warmer," Frevisse said.

"I'll be wetter!" Sister Emma returned sharply. "I don't want to be wetter. I want to be dry. And warm. We simply can't stay here. You know we can't."

"You wanted to help Nicholas. This is part of it."

"I want to help him from *indoors*. Perhaps we should have gone with Master Naylor."

This was Sister Emma at her most tedious, and worse because there was no cure for it. Frevisse could neither give her her own way nor force on her the Rule of silence, one of the mercies of the nunnery. So she tried to woo her with, "But this is an adventure. Adventures always have to be at least a little uncomfortable or who would know you'd had one? Think what you'll be able to tell when we're back in St. Frideswide's. You've stayed among outlaws and sustained us with your prayers. That's more than even Dame Alys has done." Dame Alys was St. Frideswide's ferocious kitchener, a lady who daunted almost everyone who came in her reach. "And all to save a man in peril of his life and soul."

Sister Emma stared up at her, wiping at her nose and shivering slightly, but flattered by so exalted a view of what she was doing. Firming her little mouth, she said, "I'll pray, for all of us."

"And so will I," Frevisse said. But not near Sister Emma, she added to herself as Sister Emma bent her head over her clasped hands, sniffing and murmuring.

Frevisse meant to go back to their shelter to see if there was still a dry corner where she could sit. It was surely time for the morning's office of Tierce. But Evan called to her from another leafy lean-to near her own.

"If it please you, come here, my lady, you'll find this more dry than most."

The rain was thickening; Frevisse's hesitation was hardly longer than the glance that told her that her own shelter was dripping freely all through its roof. She turned aside and ducked under Evan's.

He was sitting at one side on the end of a blanket-covered pile of straw. He nodded her to the other end of the pile and went on touching the strings of the lute he held as she sank gratefully down. The straw was nearly fresh, the blanket clean, his shelter certainly drier than anywhere else Frevisse had been today.

Evan nodded welcome without speaking, too busy tuning his lute, an instrument singularly sensitive to damp. He moved from tuning to formless playing, as if waiting for a tune to come to his fingers. It seemed part of the forest sounds of rain on leaves and hush of trees around them. Frevisse realized she had been hearing it behind her thoughts while she walked and while she talked with Sister Emma, but she could not have said when it began.

"Do you know where Nicholas is?"

"No, my lady."

"Do you know when I'm to write the letter to my uncle?"

"Ah," he said, and his fingers went still. "There is just a little problem with that."

"What sort of problem?"

"I brought the vellum, ink, and pens, but Nicholas thought it safer they be kept in his own hut. And that was a mistake, for last night the rain leaked in and—" He paused. "Do you know how to dry vellum?"

Frevisse nearly laughed at his rueful face. She shook her head and said, "Sister Emma is not going to be amused at this further delay."

Evan's fingers went back to playing as he said with a nod at Sister Emma, "She's not as happy with the carefree life of the forest as she was last night?"

"Last night was dry."

Evan smiled. Like the rest of his uneven face, it was a crooked smile and difficult to read. "Is she ailing?"

"Only complaining."

"And you're not."

"I've been wet before and have learned that I'll be dry again sometime and that until then there's no point in spending effort on complaining. Are you more peddler or outlaw?"

Evan took the change of subject with hardly a pause of his fingers on the lute strings. "More peddler, I hope," he answered.

"Have you robbed with them? Or only gathered the information that sets them on their way?"

"Robbed?" Evan showed amusement at the word. "We don't do anything so base—and perilous—as that. Not for a long while past."

"You just live merrily in the greenwood, poaching an occasional deer."

"Alas, not quite so simply as that either." He hesitated. "But those are the questions you're going to ask and want answers for before you write to your uncle, aren't they?"

Frevisse nodded. They were indeed, and since Nicholas was not to hand, Evan's answers would do for a beginning.

He had stopped playing. Now he looked down at one of his hands laid aside on his knee. A large hand, thickened across the knuckles, dark and rough with years of raw weather and hard work. "I used to have some skill at the lute, but haven't the hands for it any more." He turned his head to look at Frevisse. "We're most of us like that here. Not comfortable at what we're doing, not able to go back to what we were."

"You were a minstrel?"

Evan grinned his sideways grin. "Not quite. But it's not me you want answers for. It's Nicholas."

"You don't want pardon too?"

"Oh, very much. But Nicholas is the pivot point. If he receives pardon, we do too."

"So what do you do, if you're not robbers anymore?"

"We gather gifts."

Frevisse took a moment to absorb that idea, then asked, "From whom? For what?"

"From those well able to afford them. They pay us and we see to it that no one else takes anything from them that they don't want to give. They pay us and we protect them. This is one of the safest parts of the realm."

"You require folk to pay you not to rob them? I think the definition of 'rob' is strained a little there."

"For what they pay us—and it's only modest sums from each, well within what they can afford—we see to it that neither we nor anyone else offends their property or person."

"No robbers but yourselves within your territory. Very apt. How far does Nicholas's 'influence' spread?"

Evan shrugged, and slid away from the question. "Far enough."

"And your part is to go about as a seeming-peddler . . ."

"Indeed I am a peddler. And good at it."

"I remember. What use old Ela at the priory may have for green ribbons I cannot imagine, but you sold them to her."

"Sold her one, gave her the other. She'll never wear them, I doubt, but they'll glad her heart just because she has them."

"And that matters to you?" Frevisse said, surprised.

Evan touched his lutestrings in a tuneless, ragged run of notes. "There's little enough gladness in the world. I'll not begrudge it to anyone, and assuredly not so small a corner of it."

"But still, while going about your peddler's ways, you spy and judge who would be likely to pay for Nicholas's 'protection,' yes?"

"Indeed yes. And I keep an eye around for any who may need to be warned off our territory. And advise which of our men should be sent where when time comes for collecting, that we not set up a pattern too easily guessed at."

"In other words, Nicholas commands but it's through you that he knows what orders to give."

Evan made a small gesture of agreement.

"Evan!" one of the outlaws called from the edge of the clearing. "Nicholas wants you. Come."

"If you'll pardon me?" Evan set his lute aside into a length of waxed canvas and wrapped it around for protection from the wet day, then ducked from the shelter and left Frevisse to her own thoughts.

By midday those thoughts had turned to worry. The persistent wet and chill had finally driven her to keep Sister Emma company by the fire, along with a huddle of outlaws. Now, as the day went by, it was becoming plain that Sister Emma was not imagining the depth of her discomfort. She could no longer breathe easily, and she huddled and shivered over the fire, complaining that she hurt; and when

Frevisse ventured to lay a hand on her forehead below her wimple band, her skin was hot with fever.

That was sufficient. Frevisse went purposefully in search of Nicholas, and found him beyond the rough bushes that hid one clearing from another. He was seated with Evan on logs under another canvas shelter, and by the looks on their faces as they saw her, they had been talking about her. As they both rose and bowed to her, she ignored Nicholas's greeting and said, "Sister Emma needs to be taken somewhere she can be warm and dry and nursed. Her cold has worsened into fever and will surely go to her lungs if she stays here longer."

Nicholas hesitated.

More forcefully Frevisse said, "We don't want her death on our hands. There'll be no pardon for you in that."

Evan leaned to whisper in Nicholas's ear. Nicholas, diverted from Frevisse, looked at him disbelievingly and started to protest. Evan cut him off with, "By your leave, lady," to Frevisse, and drew Nicholas aside.

Shivering a little, Frevisse moved nearer to the fire. It was larger than the one in the other clearing, with a better pile of drier logs beside it. At the far side of the shelter Evan spoke vigorously but too low for Frevisse to hear. Then Nicholas answered him, with more question than protest now, Frevisse thought, wishing she could hear what they were saying. Evan spoke again and this time, at the end, Nicholas nodded. When he came toward her, Evan behind him, he was smiling.

Sweeping her a low bow, he said, "Your need is my command. Give me an hour, or maybe a little more, and there will be all you ask for and more."

Frevisse looked past him to where Evan nodded in confirmation. Warm with relief, she said, "Then I'll thank you most greatly, cousin."

With only a little more farewell, Nicholas left, taking one

of his men with him. Frevisse picked up an armful of the dry logs and returned to Sister Emma's fire.

Later, Evan brought them cold venison and hunks of soggy bread and mugs of ale. Frevisse ate willingly, but Sister Emma only shook her head. "I can't," she whimpered. "Everything hurts. And I can't breathe."

The fact that her words stopped there instead of running on increased Frevisse's worry. When Nicholas finally returned, she sprang to her feet in relief. He cast a frowning glance at Sister Emma. "She's no better?"

"She's worse. What have you brought?"

"Not brought. Found. But you'll have to ride."

"How far?" She doubted Sister Emma would be able to travel much.

"Four miles maybe. But there's a house at the end of it, dry beds and warm food and folk to see to her. It's an easy ride, and we can haste once we're to the road."

"Then let's go as soon as may be. She's worsening, I think."

Sister Emma barely protested when Nicholas, finally realizing she was not even good for walking, picked her up and carried her. Wet branches whipped and spattered them; rain dripped from leaves overhead; the ground squelched underfoot. Frevisse was soaked through to the skin when finally they came out on the wide way where the horses were tied, and Sister Emma was surely no better.

Hal was waiting. As Nicholas put Sister Emma down on her feet, she swayed and said pathetically, "I feel awful. And now I'm wet clear through. And *cold*."

"She can't ride alone," Frevisse said, putting an arm around her to steady her. Sister Emma sagged against her, crying softly.

"You, Hal," Nicholas said quickly. "Take her horse and I'll hand her up."

Hal, looking harassed, handed Frevisse the other reins,

hesitated over how to manage Sister Emma's box saddle, and finally swung up awkwardly behind it.

"Oh, this isn't right at all," Sister Emma moaned as Nicholas took her by the waist and heaved her up into her seat. "I can't ride with a man."

"We're taking you somewhere you'll be warm," Frevisse reassured her as she tossed her reins to Nicholas. He mounted, and she quickly swung up to sit behind the saddle.

On the highway again, where they could ride on the grassy verge, they cantered. The rain had finally eased, but the day's chill was deepening and the heavy overcast made the hour seem later than early afternoon. Sister Emma collapsed against Hal, sunk too far in misery even to notice the impropriety of leaning against a man. Frevisse kept silent behind Nicholas, yearning to urge the pace. And not soon, but sooner than she had set herself to endure, Nicholas said, "A quarter mile now maybe. Not more."

She stirred herself to look around. They were entering a village, the houses shuttered, eaves dripping, no one in sight in the muddy street. Frevisse would have been willing for this to be their goal. Even the down-at-the-corners alehouse with its bush thrust out over the street looked inviting after the rude camp in the woods. As they rode past, the half-open door gave a glimpse of firelight and a crowded room, and a drift of hot, ale-scented air wafted to them.

"Beyond the village?" she asked.

"Not far. You'll be made comfortable there. Master Payne likes his comforts and has the money for it, so you'll lack nothing."

"He knows about you?"

"We do business together, clear and honest. I told you I've not broken the law these three years. But I have to live somehow, and he's my way. Don't go asking questions about me because he won't have the answers. We're friends enough he'll do this for me, and send a messenger to

Thomas Chaucer with your letter when you've written it."

"He's agreed to all this? How did you explain Sister Emma and me being in your 'keeping'?"

Nicholas shrugged. "He's not to home right now, so I didn't need to explain."

"You persuaded his people to take us in despite him being gone?"

"Persuaded his wife. She knows I have dealings with him, and doesn't have to talk things to death to understand them like some do. Here's the turning."

As the highway swung leftward, a smaller road turned right. Another hundred yards or so along that byway they came in sight of a half-timbered gatehouse set in a low wall running between outbuildings. They were expected; a man was there to pull the gate open as they approached. He stood aside to let them pass and pushed it shut behind them as they rode on into the manor yard.

The house across the yard rose a little higher than its surroundings. Half-timbered like the gatehouse, white-plastered over its daub between the rain-darkened timbers, it was two storeys its entire, four-bay length. A plain house, but ample. And new, Frevisse guessed. Built within the last ten years, with glass in some of the upper windows. And there were at least three fireplaces; their smoking chimneys rose above the far side of the roof. Warmth and food were very near to hand.

Their coming had been watched for from the house too. The door was opened as they reached the porchless front door and servants came out to hold the horses. Hal lifted Sister Emma to the ground, and Frevisse slipped down from behind Nicholas. Sister Emma feverishly brushed away Hal's hands and collapsed against Frevisse, coughing from somewhere deep in her chest. Frevisse, praying this was not as bad as it was beginning to seem, urged her toward the door.

A woman waited a step safely back inside, away from the rain. She was small in height and bones, a little woman with a worried face, dressed in an old gown faded to a soft blue-lavender under a plain, sensible apron. But her hair and neck were covered by a white, full wimple and starched, layered veils which like her dress were of good linen. Frevisse guessed she was Mistress Payne even before she spoke in a quick, fluttered voice. "Enter, my ladies, and be welcome. We've a room all readied for you. And dry clothing. Please, come in."

Her gaze went over Frevisse's shoulder to Nicholas, still sitting on his horse in the rain. "And you'll . . . come in?" she asked. She seemed uncertain if she wanted him to accept her invitation.

Nicholas shook his head. "I've matters to see to. Tell Master Payne I'll see him when he's back." He looked at Frevisse questioningly.

Frevisse nodded. "I'll write as soon as I have chance. Tomorrow surely if not today."

Nicholas nodded back his satisfaction and gestured to Hal to mount behind him. Frevisse opened her mouth to protest. They were taking her horse. But she remained quiet. It was too much trouble; it might make too much trouble. As the two men rode away, and a servant led Sister Emma's horse toward the stables, Frevisse gratefully gave Sister Emma over to a servant woman waiting to take her, and turned her own attention to Mistress Payne.

Chapter
6

THERE WERE HALF a score of village men crowded in the Wheatsheaf, the village alehouse, this rainy afternoon. So early in the summer, men would rather have been in their fields, seeing to the weeding of the winter corn, or else in their cottage gardens tending to their lesser crop. Or even in the barns, threshing the last of the past year's harvest. But the year had been cold and wet, and what little wheat or barley or oats there had been was long since gone. There was nothing in the barns to thresh, nor much left in the way of livestock. Talk was that if this year went on as it had begun—more rainy days than dry and hardly enough sun to bring the seed up—then next winter there would be hunger even deeper than the last.

"I've to spend what good weather there is in the fields. There's not been dry days enough to let me mend my roof, and the thatch is that beaten down there's rain come through t'loft at back," one thin-shouldered man complained to his fellows.

There were general nods of gloomy sympathy among his benchmates near the hearth.

"Still," one man noted, "it's not like you'd aught there to be getting wet. Excepting floorboards. Unless you've more set away than the rest of us."

"I've as much in my loft as you've in your head. So it's empty enough."

Laughter grumbled around the circle. In a corner obscured in the haze of smoke that swirled down from the smoke hole and the lights set here and there around the room, Nicholas sat with his hands wrapped around a second pot of ale. "Poor old gabbers, their brains reach no higher than their weeds or farther than their hedgerows."

"It's life or death to them, after all," Evan said, his first pot hardly tasted. "And to us, for that matter. We eat the bread their grain grows for. Or don't eat if it doesn't grow."

"There's always bread for the rich. And so long as the rich have bread, so do the likes of us. We've better ways to life and death, and more certain profit at the end of it than these poor fools. Here's to our pardons."

The men touched the rims of their mugs together. The Wheatsheaf did not run to better than cheap pottery, but the alewife never watered her brew, and no one ever asked much about Nicholas or any of his men when they came there. Otherwise, it was no more than a small and dirty village alehouse, with nothing else to recommend it— except Beatrice. She had come that way a few years back and stayed on because she had nowhere better to go, and Old Nan, the alewife, needed a sturdy serving wench now that she was not so young herself. The two women got on well enough, and Beatrice got on with any of the village men who fancied her and had a few pence to pay for it.

Now she came carrying a jug toward Nicholas and Evan out of the fug of ale and smoke. She was a wide-hipped, ample-breasted woman with a froth of fair hair that hazed around her uncovered head. Her age was hard to tell, but her first youth was gone; a sag was overtaking her softness and there were lines in her fair skin that had not been there a while ago. But she was still a woman worth his having, and good-humored in the bargain; and while she took pence from the other men, she was always Nicholas's for the asking. Not that he did not gift her handsomely from time to time, as fortune favored him.

He wrapped an arm around her rump, grinning up at her as she bent to pour his ale. She smiled back, leaning into his hold, resting a soft breast against his shoulder.

"Will you bide the night?" she asked. "I know where there's a dry bed you're welcome to warm."

"And no bed I'd rather," Nicholas answered. "But Evan is of a mind the men will take it ill if they're left in the rain while I lie easy, so I'd best be back. We've something afoot and I need them happy."

"You need me happy too." Beatrice leaned nearer, smelling warm and womanly. Nicholas ran his hand down to her hem and under the edge of her dress to her ankle and began to work his way up.

Evan reached past him to take the ale jug and pour his own mug full. "What's Will Colfoot doing here? That's him in the corner, isn't it, with the other fellow I don't know?"

Not bothering to look around, Beatrice said, "That's him, and his yeoman. Doesn't bother with the likes of this place often, but happens he's making his monthly circuit and tired of the rain."

While his hand went on with its business, Nicholas looked past her to the other corner. "Will Colfoot? I don't know him, do I? Who is he?"

"A franklin from along toward Burford and other places round about."

"A franklin?" Nicholas looked at Evan with roused interest. "One of ours?"

"No. He's not safe. He has a temper, and a nasty way with anyone who crosses him so much as a breadth of a nail-head," Evan answered.

Nicholas returned his attention to Colfoot. "But if he's a franklin, the inside of his purse knows what coins look like, sure as sinning. What do you know about him, Beatrice? How much does he carry when he travels, and how many servants are with him?"

Evan stirred uneasily, but Beatrice leaned more heavily into Nicholas, still trying to hold his attention while she answered, "He carries enough to keep him comfortable, and he likes his comforts. He has a single yeoman with him always. That's the fellow at the table with him. They're both armed, and don't you be thinking of making trouble here. Old Nan values her reputation."

"And Lord knows she's had one in her day," Nicholas jibed. "From what tales I've heard tell—"

Beatrice poked him warmly in the ribs and sat down on his thigh. "I'd not be mentioning those tales where she could hear you. She still has an arm that can set a man's ear to ringing if she gets a clear swing." She settled in closer, her softness pressing against him. "Now you kiss me and not be looking at a fat old franklin or I'll think your fancy's straying."

She proceeded then—with Nicholas willing—to make sure she was the only thing he was noticing, until Old Nan squealed at her from the kitchen doorway to shift herself, that there were others that paid more and needed waiting on. With a final smothering kiss, Beatrice obliged. Nicholas's attention went back to Will Colfoot.

"One yeoman, a fat franklin, and a fatter purse. That's easy pluckings."

"That's a fool's wishful thinking!" Evan retorted, but softly. "They're both armed. The yeoman is taller than you and younger than either of us. And that bulk across Colfoot's shoulders looks more muscle than fat to me."

"Then one hale yeoman and a not-so-fat franklin," Nicholas returned. "The point is, his purse is fat, for a surety. You don't dress in burgundy wool if you're pressed for coin, and that's as fine a stretch of cloth he's wearing as I've seen this many a day."

"Nicholas, these are our home roads. You'd not be such a fool as to stir trouble on them. We need no hue and cry after us, nor to risk our pardons at this near date."

Nicholas valued Evan's cleverness. But cleverness that interfered with sport was boring. Nicholas jammed his elbow into Evan's arm. "Why don't you ever have a go at Beatrice? She's a willing armful. Take some of that stiffness out of your backbone and put it lower, where it'll do you some good."

Evan glanced aside at him. His expression was edged with a variety of answers, but he made none of them. After a moment staring away down into the darkness of his ale, he asked, "Your cousin will still write the letter to Chaucer, now she's out from under your hand?"

Nicholas made a dismissive sound. "She'll write it. She's given her word, and her neck is as stiff as yours when she's pledged herself to something. I remember that much about her. Lord!" Nicholas snorted. "A nun. That suits her."

"How do you mean?"

"Because when I knew her the little while I was in Chaucer's household—and a duller place you wouldn't want to be abandoned in—she and her uncle were enough of a matched set to curdle your blood. So fond of their own wits that nobody else could abide their cleverness. No, she'll keep her word now she's given it. She's too proud to do otherwise. They're as proud a pair as you'll find this side of the king's court, she and her uncle." Nicholas's voice had a bitter edge.

"So maybe she went to God because she couldn't stomach orders from anyone less," Evan suggested with a grin.

Nicholas laughed out loud. "Aye. You've probably the right of it there." He fixed Evan with a look. "What do you care about her anyway?"

"She's our way to Chaucer and out of here. I want to know how sure we can be of her."

"If the thing can be done, she'll do it." Nicholas took a long quaff of the ale. "By Christmas I'll be an honest man, with the greenwood and my merry men far behind me. You certain sure you don't want to be leader after me? You've a knack for the life."

"I've a knack for other things too, and most of them safer. Besides, the pardon is for all the band. There'll be no more 'merry men.'"

"Faugh, you know them better than that. Most of them haven't the wit for anything better. Left to their own, they'll be back where they are before the year turns, pardon or no pardon. And without my brains to see them along, they'll be pudding for crows by next Christmas. Unless you take them on."

Evan shook his head. "I'm done. We each of us have enough money put by to set ourselves up decently. Now's the time to do it, before our luck runs out."

"Luck?" Nicholas scoffed. "A man makes his own luck. Was any of this with Frevisse luck? It was planning that did it, and my wit in handling her. And look how I've handled Payne. We'd not be where we are now if it wasn't for my wit in that."

Evan looked at him soberly. He had drunk far less than Nicholas; he always did. His soberness was among the things Nicholas found hard to abide. Evan was useful, worth keeping friends with, but dog-dull in more ways than one. And hard to fathom. He kept too many of his thoughts shut up behind that crooked face. And now, when Nicholas was expecting him to say something else, he said instead, "We'd best be off if we're to be back at camp by dark. Even afoot, Hal will be there by now."

"Then let Hal tell them we've not gone astray. I've a

mind to that warm bed Beatrice offered me after all. You go on if you've a mind to but I'm staying."

Evan rose. "You said you'd be coming back."

"And I will. Just not so soon. I'll be there by dark."

Evan glanced across the room and said, as if it followed naturally, "You let the franklin be."

"Soul's honor!" Nicholas exclaimed. "He's not for my touching. Now get along with you. I can find my way from here to there without your old-maid fussing at me."

Master Payne's house was in the new fashion. Frevisse, even burdened with Sister Emma, saw that much as they were brought into the great hall, a long, broad room meant to be the gathering place of the household. Time had been when every hall had been tall, open to the high peak of the roof, but this one was ceilinged. It made the room less grand but warmer; and instead of an open hearth in the midst of the floor, there was a wide fireplace on the farther wall, built up with a goodly fire. Stools had been set there for them, and Sister Emma sank down on one gratefully, hiccuping a few sobs of relief as she held out her hands, white with cold, to the heat.

Mistress Payne had clearly had some thought of playing hostess to them, but Sister Emma's condition was too poor. She asked in a worried tone, "Do you think it might be better if you went straight to the room we're readying for you? I think she's more than merely chilled. She's sickening for something, isn't she?"

Watching Sister Emma shiver and huddle nearer the fire, Frevisse nodded. "I fear so. Is the room warm?"

"Oh, very warm, yes. It's private too, with its own fireplace and a fire already going." There was more worry than pride in that, as if Mistress Payne feared Frevisse might disapprove of the extravagance.

Far from disapproval, Frevisse said, "That will be wonderful. Thank you." At St. Frideswide's, only the prioress's parlor and the warming room had fireplaces, and their use was very limited. A private room with a fireplace was luxury, and just now she was in no mood to consider how far from the Rule it might be for her even here. She took Sister Emma around the shoulders and by the arm and urged her to her feet. "Come, Sister. We have someplace better for you."

Coughing heavily against her sleeve, Sister Emma resisted, still keeping her free hand out to the fire. "But I like it here," she protested. "This feels so *wonderful*."

"We have someplace more wonderful," Frevisse insisted. "With a fireplace just as warm. Where you can be rid of your wet clothes and have dry ones." She glanced at Mistress Payne, who nodded agreement. "And a bed too. So come. It's only a little farther."

"H-he that was b-born to be hanged sh-shall never be drowned," Sister Emma chattered. But she let Frevisse, with Mistress Payne on her other side, manage her to her feet. She was shivering uncontrollably now. "I'm n-never going to be w-warm again, I know it," she whispered, leaning more heavily on Frevisse with every step.

"You're going to be warm again very soon. And dry. You just have to go a little way."

"Hope long deferred makes the heart sick," Sister Emma offered.

"This won't take long," Frevisse said. So long as Sister Emma could still drag out proverbs, she was not beyond hope. "But you have to walk. There's no one here can carry you."

Mistress Payne, looking all worry edged with nervousness, led them back into the screens passage at the end of the hall, where the tall, carved wooden screen sheltered the hall from the drafts of main and back doors. They had entered from its left end, where the main door opened to the foreyard of the manor. Now they turned right, went past the door to the kitchen where a drift of good smells gave hope of supper to come, to another doorway and the narrow darkness of a spiral staircase upward to another floor.

"I'm so c-cold," Sister Emma chattered.

"So am I," Frevisse agreed. "But if you keep walking, we'll be warm soon enough. Up now."

Even if there had been someone to carry her, they could not have done it up those narrow stairs, except over the shoulder like a bag of grain. With difficulty and despite Emma's insistent helplessness, Frevisse and Mistress Payne managed her, emerging at the top into a long, narrow room that ran from where they were to the front of the house. Its further end was curtained off into a small chamber where Frevisse glimpsed a bed and writing desk. There were also doors to either side; Mistress Payne, panting with nervousness and exertion, led them right, to the door nearest the stairhead.

"My sister-in-law's chamber," she said. "Poor Magdalen was widowed three years ago, and came to live with us. Her room's the most private we have. All her own. None of the rest of the family sleeps here. You'll be very comfortable. And when I can't see to you myself, Magdalen will. She's very sweet."

From Mistress Payne's hurried explanation, Frevisse was picturing a widow sunk well into middle age, her children grown and herself so worn that she was willing to live with her brother rather than manage her life herself. But at the word "sweet," she swung her expectation to a very young woman unfit to live on her own.

The reality was a woman perhaps in her thirties who, as they entered, straightened from helping a servant spread a sheet across the tall bed whose curtains were tied open. She looked at them from where she stood at the far end of the room with a long, clear gaze before coming to meet them.

There was no way to tell the color of her hair under the encompassing wimple and veil she wore, but her brows were dark and her eyes rain-gray. Her dress was modest—a dark green gown with plain high neckline and straight sleeves, unwaisted but quietly shaped to her hips before flaring to full skirts. She was tall for a woman, though not quite Frevisse's height, and she moved with grace and reserve together as she came to take the weight of Sister Emma's other side from Mistress Payne. "These are the nuns, Magdalen," Mistress Payne said in haste. "Dame Frevisse"—Frevisse and Magdalen exchanged a quick, acknowledging look over Sister Emma's sinking head— "and Sister Emma, who's ill, I'm afraid. Can you—there's still supper to see to and I don't know when Oliver will be here or what he'll say—I want to be the one to tell him. Could you . . . ?"

"I'll see to them, gladly." Magdalen's voice was low-pitched and even. The house was Mistress Payne's, and Magdalen was younger, but she spoke with the kind, amused firmness of an older sister. "The bed is near to ready, you can see; and Maud has found dry gowns for them; and there's spiced wine heating on the hearth. You can be at ease about it all. Leave them to me and go to your duties."

"It's Oliver—he doesn't know yet, and when he does . . ."

"He'll be startled. And then he'll be glad of his chance to do these ladies courtesy. His heart is as good as yours, Iseult, and he understands necessity as well as you do. There'll be no trouble. Now go on."

Magdalen smiled reassuringly; and after an uncertain moment Mistress Payne took a deep breath and, with a quick curtsy to Frevisse and at Sister Emma, left.

Chapter
☙ 7 ❧

THE RAINY DARK had drawn in early, and the shutters were closed against the chill. Most of the room was in shadow, save for the firelight and the small golden glow of the lamp set near where Sister Emma now lay, breathing heavily in her sleep. It was a large chamber, the width of the house at its gabled end. There were a standing loom near the window, a single chair close to the hearth, chests along the walls, and a few short stools.

Frevisse sat on the chair dressed now in a plain, dark blue gown of one of Magdalen's serving women and enjoying being warm, dry, and well-fed. She had dined on saffron rice with figs and her hands were wrapped around a mug of spiced, hot wine, her second from the pitcher keeping warm near the fire. But her mind was not completely at rest. The unfamiliarity was unsettling. To sit at ease, warm with wine, in a comfortable chair, at an hour when she would normally have been in her bed in St. Frideswide's dormitory sleeping toward midnight Matins and Lauds. To be wearing under-garments and a gown that despite their plainness revealed her body far more than the enveloping, unvarying familiarity of her Benedictine habit. And to have her short-cropped hair uncovered to finish drying in the fire's warmth. Except for when the nunnery had hair washing and hair cutting, her head had been covered by wimple and veil all day, every day, since she had entered St. Frideswide's as a novice in her young womanhood. Now she felt vaguely indecent because of her head's nakedness. And uneasily pleasured at such unfamiliar comfort and ease.

Across the hearth from her, seated on a stool, Magdalen had uncovered her own head and was combing down her waist-long hair in readiness for bed. The firelight caught and glittered on her silver comb and found pale strands among the dark brown. Her hair would be beautiful all her life, Frevisse thought; it would not dull or fade but turn white with the years and still be beautiful, as would her face, whose fine bones would hold their beauty too with passing time. Frevisse wondered why she had not married again. Had she been so much in love with her first husband that three years of widowhood had not dimmed the pain of losing him?

Or had he been so harsh that she dreaded taking a second husband?

She did not want to ask, though she and Magdalen had been easy with each other from the very first, Magdalen's quiet competence setting so well with Frevisse's own bolder way that they had worked almost wordlessly together in stripping Sister Emma of her wet clothing, dressing her in a linen shift for extra warmth, and putting her to bed under many blankets. Then Magdalen had had one of her women brew an herbal posset, and Frevisse and she had forced Sister Emma to drink it, and under its influence Sister Emma had subsided to murmuring drowsiness and then sleep.

Darkness had come while they were about it; and then supper had been brought; and now they were sitting together by the hearth in the companionable silence of shared tasks well done and a friendship begun.

Concentrating on a small tangle resisting her comb, Magdalen asked in her gentle way, "Is there anything else you want or need?"

"Nothing else at all except bed and I'll go there shortly." When Sister Emma was deep enough asleep not to rouse Frevisse crawled in beside her. "I've been most marvelously seen to. But we're taking your bed. Where will you sleep?"

"There," Magdalen said, nodding across the room toward the two truckle beds already drawn out from under the foot of her own. "My maidservant Maud will join the other servants in the hall and I shall have her bed. Bess will stay, to be at hand."

"We're giving you a great deal of trouble."

"It's trouble well-bestowed to a good end," Magdalen answered with a smile. "And more an honor than trouble, come to that. Truly, I'm glad to have you here."

"You've lived here with your brother's family three years, I think Mistress Payne said."

"Three years almost to the month," Magdalen agreed. "They've been very kind to me."

"But you've no mind to have your own home again?"

"Or to marry?" Magdalen completed the thought with only the slightest of smiles. She turned her head sideways, bringing her hair forward, to curtain her face and reach nearly to the floor as she continued combing. "No. I was married full many years to John Dow, beginning when I was fourteen. I enjoyed being a wife, but I've found I also enjoy being unmarried. And there's a certain pleasure in being responsible for very little, as I am here under my brother's roof. And by my brother's advice, I've given most of my properties to rent. He manages them for me, at a pleasant profit to us both, and I live here, sometimes a help to Iseult and always a fond aunt to her little ones."

Earlier, before full dark, Frevisse had seen the door open ever so slightly and two small heads—a boy and a girl, she thought but it was difficult to tell in the shadows—had peered around the edge. She had said nothing, and they had quickly withdrawn as silently as they had come.

"How many Payne children are there?"

"Five." Magdalen straightened and threw her hair back over her shoulder. "Though Edward would be wrathful to hear himself described as a child. He's all of fifteen and has been at university this year and a half past. He's to be a lawyer at the Inns of Court when he's finished at Oxford. He's home now for a month, and except he's gone with his father, he would have greeted you at the door as man of the house."

She said it with such a combination of amusement and warm sympathy that Frevisse asked, "Is he your favorite?"

Magdalen shook her head. "I know better than to have a favorite. I like each for who each is. They're all too different from one another. And poor Edward is in a difficult time just now, so aware that he's the eldest and the heir, since Edmund died. But he's only fifteen and not a man yet, for all he thinks he should be. There was some talk he should give up the law, after his older brother died, but Edward's too good at his studies to settle for less than what the law can bring him. He'll find his balance in a little while. But meanwhile he can be . . ."

She paused, looking for the word.

"Prickly?" Frevisse offered.

Magdalen smiled. "I mustn't say so. But his brother Richard is surely an easier person to be with. He's always been the quiet one, but his judgment's steady. He's twelve and shares Edward's room if not Edward's love of learning. And then there's Katherine. She's nine, and much the young image of her mother and a darling."

Darling was not a word Frevisse would have chosen for Mistress Payne, but Magdalen's fondness for both her sister-in-law and niece was plain.

"And then there's Kate—another Katherine because her sister was sickly when Kate was born and Oliver wanted to be sure to keep our mother's name among his children. She's a darling, too, in her own way. And then there's Bartholomew. He and Kate are rascals; they work together to their own ends more often than not, and God save the rest of us when they do. They seem to take especial pleasure in tormenting Edward because he's just at the age to feel his dignity most tenderly." She smiled again. "Last week they—"

A tapping at the door interrupted her. She called, "Come," and Mistress Payne opened the door barely enough to slip through. She pushed it closed behind her, then hurried over to bob a curtsy to Frevisse and say earnestly, "My husband has returned and begs the favor of seeing you, to assure you of his welcome. Is it possible? Are you . . . ?" She gestured vaguely to cover the myriad possible reasons Frevisse might have for refusing.

To Frevisse's mind it would be discourtesy to refuse to meet her host. And she was curious too to meet someone who had supposedly honest dealings with Nicholas. She quickly said, "I'd be very pleased to see him. To thank him and—" She broke off, her hand going to her bare head and then to her gown. She was not dressed for being seen by any man.

But Magdalen had already risen and gone to one of the chests along the wall to bring back a wimple and veil of her own. "Here," she said. "They're not like your own but they might do." She went to another chest and brought out a dark cloak. "And this will cover your gown."

The wimple and veil were most assuredly not like Frevisse's own; the linen was woven far finer than any they wore in St. Frideswide's, and she had not worn a white veil since she was a novice.

"Pins," Magdalen said, and went to fetch them, then

arranged the wimple to cover Frevisse's forehead, throat, and chin. She pinned it in place and the veil over it. "There! And here's the cloak."

As Magdalen draped the cloak around her shoulders, Frevisse felt its sumptuous soft wool and its squirrel-fur lining. Trying to ignore how elegant it felt, she glanced across the room at Sister Emma, still soundly sleeping. Iseult, following her thought, went to close the bed curtains. Magdalen stepped back from making sure the cloak covered her down to her toes and said, "Yes, you'll do very well. I doubt even your prioress could object. Let him come in now, Iseult."

Frevisse rose, and her hands moved to tuck themselves up either sleeve in a familiar gesture. But the gown fitted too close to her wrists. Feeling the lack of her habit's dignity more than she would have expected, she made do with folding her hands in front of her as Mistress Payne hastened out the door.

The man who entered a few moments later had Magdalen's height and her rich dark hair. But he was older, with the solid build of a man going into successful middle age, and with more gray in his hair. He had done his guests the honor of washing and changing before he came to see them; he wore a rich, wide-belted gown of soft crimson wool, well-fitted hosen, and red leather shoes in which he clearly had not traveled.

Although there was correct courtesy in his bearing as he crossed to Frevisse and bowed to her, there was also assured pride as he said in a deep, even, pleasant voice, "My lady, my greetings and my gladness that you're here."

"Master Payne," Frevisse returned, with a slight curtsy to his bow. "We owe you a great thanks for your hospitality."

"My pleasure that we're able to serve you." He looked toward the bed. "The other sister sleeps?"

"By God's mercy and Magdalen's kindness. Sleep is the best thing for her chill, I think."

"You both have everything you need?"

"In abundance, I assure you. We're well cared for."

He turned to Magdalen. "If there's anything you need, send someone for it immediately."

Magdalen smiled reassuringly. "I will. How was the day?"

"Well enough except for the rain. That made it tedious. But the child is christened and the dinner was ample and the company good. And it seems the message was true that said the expected godmother was safe but delayed."

Frevisse startled. "You were at the Pellow christening?"

Master Payne laughed aloud, then caught himself with a little bow of apology. "Yes. I think you were supposed to be? I'm in the presence of the missing godmother?"

Frevisse found herself smiling back at him. She nodded toward the bed. "Yes. Sister Emma was to be godmother, and I was traveling with her. They found someone else? Master Naylor arrived with his message in good time?"

"The mother stood proxy for Sister Emma. There seemed to be a general feeling that—since they were assured of her safety—it was more exciting than alarming that the god-mother was—uh—delayed on the way. The Pellows will make a story out of that for some time to come."

If the rest of the Pellow family were anything like Sister Emma, Frevisse could readily believe that. In fact, Frevisse already had an uncomfortable suspicion that when they were finally home again, recreation times at St. Frides-wide's were going to be full of Sister Emma's recitation of this adventure for far longer than Frevisse was going to want to listen.

"Master Naylor, our nunnery steward—he was safe?" she asked.

Master Payne inclined his head. "I assume he was. He had come and gone before Edward and I arrived."

And had undoubtedly returned to St. Frideswide's to inform Domina Edith what had happened. But Master Naylor thought they were still with Nicholas in the woods.

"Would it be possible for me to send a message to my prioress?" Frevisse asked. "To let her know we're well."

Master Payne inclined his head in willing agreement. "Few things would be simpler. I can send one of my men tomorrow with anything you wish."

Master Payne's easy answer reassured her that they were not prisoners here. But it left other problems. He seemed to accept their presence here without question. Did he know what Nicholas was, and yet have dealings with him, which the law expressly forbade?

But then Nicholas had said Master Payne did not know he was an outlaw and that such dealings as they had were honest. There must be a lie there somewhere, but she did not know which way it went. Best not to say too much at present, she decided. Let it wait until morning.

"We'll leave you now," Master Payne was saying with another moderate bow. "You're sure you have all you need?"

"More than enough," Frevisse assured him.

"And the other—Sister Emma—is not very ill, you're sure? We can send for a doctor. . . ."

Frevisse shook her head. "So far it's no more than a bad chill and a heavy cough. She's resting now and should be better in the morning. I think there's no need to worry."

"Then we'll leave you to your rest. God be with you."

"And with you," Frevisse replied.

He left, and while Magdalen shut the door behind him, Frevisse moved wearily to lay the cloak on the chest where it had come from and remove the veil and wimple, careful not to lose the pins. How had she come to be in this position? Sworn to aid her outlaw cousin—to aid his whole band, come to that. Guest of a man whose honesty she had to doubt but whose womenfolk she found open and friendly. And certainly in her behavior she was stretching the limits of the Rule farther than she thought Domina Edith would accept. She had not even said Compline prayers yet and it was long past time for them.

And long past time for being in bed. Again she was aware of her own exhaustion, and aware of how welcomingly soft and deep with blankets she was expecting the bed to be. Tomorrow she would sort it out, both the questions and her feelings. Tomorrow she would follow the Rule. Tonight she simply wanted to sleep.

Chapter

❧ 8 ❧

THERE WERE SEVERAL reasons Nicholas preferred to meet with Oliver Payne in Payne's house, rather than along some road or in the forest. Not least was the fact that they could be dry and warm. Today there was a coal fire on the parlor hearth, giving off heat like a blacksmith's forge. Nicholas kept near it as he could, steam rising from his drying clothing while they spoke. He wished Payne would offer him some of the Spanish wine he knew was kept locked in the aumbry against the farther wall. And besides Spanish wine and a coal fire, the man had two elaborately carved and cushioned chairs, a woven—not painted—French tapestry showing the Fall of Troy, a mullioned glass window looking out into a lady's garden, and—God save the mark—a carpet on the floor instead of plain rush matting! Nicholas's own father had had no carpet and he had been a knight, not a jumped-up commoner like Payne. Damn him, Payne did not stint on his comforts, but Nicholas meant to match him and more when this outlawry was over.

But in the meanwhile one of the other pleasures of coming here—and not the least—was that Payne hated him to be there.

Today, dressed in a green wool houppelande with a high

standing collar and huge bagged sleeves edged with white rabbit fur, Oliver Payne made a stark contrast to Nicholas, rough in his green-brown doublet and slack hosen, worn boots, and ragged-hemmed cloak. They both felt the difference; but Nicholas, for the sake of what he wanted from Payne, was keeping his irk hidden behind smooth face and casual voice, while Payne kept as much of the room as he could between them. He stood now drumming his fingers on the locked lid of his accounts chest as he said, "This could be handled otherwise. I'm perfectly able to oversee her writing this letter. You don't need to be here. I understand what you want."

Nicholas made a dismissive gesture. "I want to be sure of what she does. This is my life at stake."

"It's your life if you're caught here, and a great deal of damage to me. There are safer ways to meet."

That was true enough; but they were not so amusing. Nicholas dragged one of the carved chairs nearer to the fire. "I thought it would still be raining today," he explained. He sat down and stretched his feet to the fire; Payne hadn't asked him to sit, but Payne was a commoner, with manners to match. "I thought you'd not care to muddy yourself coming to me."

In fact the rain had stopped in the night. This mid-morning there was watery sunshine through thin clouds, but the world was still dripping, and a damp chill permeated everything. A strong draught of Spanish wine would have gone to warm the right places, if Payne weren't such a swine as not to offer it.

Payne's disapproval was unabated. "It would be better than your coming here."

Nicholas shifted ground. "But here I am, say what we will. So while we wait for my cousin to come down, tell me how my money goes."

Making a sharp, impatient gesture, Oliver Payne turned to pace away from his accounts chest. "Well enough."

"Well enough I can live at ease in my 'retirement' when it comes?" Nicholas persisted, enjoying Payne's dislike of the subject. From what Payne had told him other times, his money had been set to good account in three merchant ventures, and profits from those had been put into a London goldsmith's keeping for further investment. Nicholas had never bothered over the details of how it was all managed; Payne was the steward, that was his business. It was enough that Payne could tell him how much he had and how much it was likely to grow into.

"If you can enjoy retiring on what you've thieved, yes, you'll be able to enjoy your pardon when it comes," Payne answered irritably.

Rubbing his hands, Nicholas laughed with unfeigned amusement. "I come by my money as honestly as the men I take it from: stewards and franklins and all their kind, who harry the common folk for great lords' gains. They all know as much about thieving as I do. As much as you know, Master Oliver Payne," he added, for sport.

Payne swung around to face him, mouth open for a retort. But he cut it off before it came.

Nicholas pressed harder. "You and your kind are the ones with the fat purses, not the rest of us. You wring farthings from villeins on behalf of their lords, and then more farthings for yourselves by every way the law allows—and every way the law can blink at: an overcharge here on some custom of the manor, a forestalling there of someone's rights. How many ways do you have of putting a profit into your own purse? How much of your profit comes from cheating the men you're steward to? You're steward to how many lords, Payne? How many manors do you play games with? More than enough, to judge by this house and what you have in it. Aren't you thankful you and I've made an agreement whereby you do me service for my protection, rather than your having to pay me outright for it?"

Payne's face was closed over whatever he was thinking, but a small muscle jumped in his cheek.

Nicholas leaned back in the chair and went on. Deprived of the Spanish wine, he would at least enjoy himself this way. "And merchants! Now they're the prettiest piece of all. How many ways have they got of bringing up their earnings? Bribing woolpackers to low-value wool before they buy it off some hapless wight. Pricing up what they offer to sell past any reason. And who knows what else? I can't regret or do penance for so much as a ha'penny had off of any of them, by highway robbery or otherwise. God send the lot of them where they deserve to go; there's not an honest pair of them in the whole kingdom! No more than you stewards—"

He was cut off from learning how much it would take to goad Payne into open anger by a light tapping at the door.

"Come," Payne said tersely.

One of his servants entered and bowed. "The lady waits in the hall, sir."

"Bid her come in, if it please her," Payne said, and as the servant withdrew, turned on Nicholas. "You've already made the mistake of bringing her here," he said in a low, hard voice. "You say you haven't told her anything except we have business together and that I don't know you're an outlaw. But she must be curious, and the more time she has to wonder, the more she may guess. So do what you want done as fast as may be, and then be gone. Those are my terms."

A hot reply rose along with Nicholas's temper, but before he could answer, the servant had returned with Frevisse and a maidservant.

Frevisse took the room in at a glance, as she came forward to curtsy to Nicholas and Master Payne. She had the impression of something unpleasant and uncompleted between them; and the looks they briefly gave each other as they straightened from their bows to her were sharp and bare of cordiality. She gave no sign of noticing, but simply went to sit on the chair Master Payne indicated.

Nicholas looked at Payne as if expecting him to tell the maidservant, Bess, to leave, but Payne of course did not. A nun must not meet alone with men.

Bess withdrew unobtrusively to the side of the now-closed door, to stand with her eyes cast down, her hands folded.

Frevisse's Benedictine habit had been laundered, dried, and well ironed before being returned to her this morning. Now that she was dressed and veiled in its familiarity, her confidence was restored. She said, "You want me to write my letter to Master Chaucer now, I suppose?"

At this blunt statement of purpose, Master Payne's eyebrows rose.

"If you'll be so good," Nicholas replied, his smile warm with charm. Frevisse noticed he had taken the trouble to shave, but supposed there had been little he could do about his clothing; the contrast of his roughness to Master Payne's assured sleekness was strong. She remembered Nicholas in his noble youth, peacock proud and always elegant.

Only his arrogance remained. She wondered at the tension between him and Master Payne. "And you'll take the letter to Master Chaucer yourself?" she asked, knowing full well he would not dare to put himself in such jeopardy.

He hesitated, his eyes gleaming at what he perceived as a challenge. Then he shrugged. "Payne has offered to send one of his men with it."

Master Payne appeared surprised.

"I also need to write to my prioress, to advise her where we are, what has happened, and that we're well."

There was something less than strict truth in that; Sister

Emma was not well. She had slept through the night but woken before dawn, feverish and choking on phlegm.

Frevisse looked around the room. "Where will you have me write?"

"You wish to do it yourself?" Master Payne asked. "Or would you rather I wrote for you?"

Frevisse smiled her thanks but answered, "I write a fair hand, thank you, and my prioress and uncle both know my writing. It will probably be best if I do it myself."

Nicholas laughed harshly at that, but said nothing.

"Then here," Master Payne said, and set out ink and pen and paper on a standing desk set near the window for best light.

Frevisse had noted and appreciated the room's furnishings when she entered. Now, as she went to the desk, she noticed that the windows had heavy shutters, and the shutters could be barred. Also, the chests along the farther wall were both metal-banded and heavily locked. This was clearly a room meant for Master Payne's business.

The three pens laid out beside the inkwell were well-trimmed, the sheet of paper she drew toward her of fine quality. Master Payne with admirable reticence stayed where he was, but Nicholas came to stand behind her shoulder and ask, "Do you want my help with what to say?"

"No." Frevisse picked up a pen, chose her words, and began the first of what would probably be several drafts. "Right worshipful and my revered and most special and esteemed good Uncle, I commend me to you in my best way. . . ."

The balance between what needed to be said and what left out was difficult, but once she had what she needed to say clear in her mind, the body of the letter came fluently. At one point, Nicholas, hovering behind her, began to interrupt, but Frevisse shook her head in a short, sharp negative and he subsided.

Still, it was more than an hour before she was reading over her final fair copy, with its closing plea, "For these reasons I beseech you to have talk with him, that you may know as I do that he is sincere in his desire and reformation. Acknowledging myself deeply bound to you for many favors and by my especial love, and having you ever in my prayers, I remain in humble reverence, your niece . . ."

She signed and dated it, straightened up, and held it out to Master Payne, who had stood waiting at the far end of the window while she wrote. With a glance at Nicholas, who shrugged indifferently, Master Payne took the letter, read it with no sign of surprise, and handed it back. One question answered: Payne knew what Nicholas was.

"It should serve very well," he said. "You can be pleased with it, Nicholas."

"Seal it then," Nicholas said impatiently, "and we'll send it."

When the letter was folded and sealed, Frevisse wrote Master Chaucer's name and "At his manor of Ewelme or wheresoever he may be" on its outside. She handed it to Master Payne and took another sheet of paper.

The letter for Domina Edith might prove more taxing than the one to her uncle, she was afraid, because she suspected that Domina Edith would have deep reservations about what she had done through the past few days and was doing now; and she needed to find a way to put it all in the best light.

But before she could begin, there was a hurried knock and, at Master Payne's "Come," one of his men entered, bowed, and said, "Will Colfoot's at the door, wanting to see you, sir. He's set up over something and says he must speak with you now, though I said you're busy."

"The hall door?" Master Payne asked.

"Yes, sir."

A look passed between Nicholas and Master Payne.

Frevisse doubted either of them wanted Nicholas seen there; and apparently this Will Colfoot was not someone who would be easily dismissed. She rose. "I had best go," she said.

Master Payne bowed. "My thanks for your understanding." His tone showing he appreciated she was not ignorant of the several layers in what was happening here; and Frevisse felt a slight warming toward him. She curtsied to him and paused on her way to the door to lay her hand on Nicholas's arm and say, "Be patient. And careful. This isn't a matter quickly accomplished. Even Uncle Thomas must have some little time to consider."

Nicholas raised her hand and kissed it. "At your command, cousin," he said, but the pressure showed on him, and Frevisse suppressed a smile. That the imperiled life of an outlaw was obviously wearing on his nerves promised some hope for his complete reform once he had pardon.

Bess, the waiting-woman, fell in behind her again as she left the room, and Master Payne's servant, after standing aside to hold the door for them, followed after on his way to bring Will Colfoot to his master. The parlor opened directly into the hall; Frevisse had to cross the width of the great room to reach the screens passage and the stairs to Magdalen's chamber. She was only three-quarters of the way when a burly man stalked through the doorway ahead of her, headed toward the parlor she had just left. Master Payne's servant made a strangled sound and hurried to circle past the women and intercept him.

The man brushed aside whatever he was about to say with a heavy gesture, declaring, "No, Jack, I'm not going to be kept waiting at the door like a beggar, and I don't need leading like a half-wit. I've been here before."

"But if you will—" Jack tried again.

Colfoot overrode his protest without slowing down.

"Whoever is with him can put their business off till later. Mine's the more important."

Clearly Colfoot considered the servant no impediment, but Nicholas needed more time to be out the window and safely away. Despite her misgivings over his behavior, Frevisse did not wish to endanger him. She stepped deliberately into Colfoot's path and said at her most charming, "Good sir, I'm afraid I'm the cause of your delay. My most humble regrets."

Too intent on his business to actually note her existence until then, Colfoot came to as abrupt a halt as his bulk allowed, looming over her. A long while since he had gone past a natural thickness of body into layers of fat laid solidly around his middle and along his jowls. Further padded out by the overly full houppelande he wore and his wide-rolled, long-liripiped hat, he was impressive for sheer size, even before his glare centered on her with the full force of his not-inconsiderable character.

He glared at her for the instant before he recognized her habit. Then his face and manners changed from heavy annoyance to a degree of respect. He pulled off his hat and bowed to her with, "Good Sister, my apologies. This fool never said who Payne was with. I thought it was business, not . . ."

He stopped, clearly at a loss why she should be with Master Payne about anything. Obligingly Frevisse said, "I was thanking Master Payne for his kindness and asking if he would send someone with a letter to my prioress." She sighed and drooped slightly with weariness. "He and his good wife gave us shelter from yesterday's rain, you know, and now Sister Emma has such a chill that we have to stay a while longer. He's such a kind man, don't you think?"

Will Colfoot was clearly not interested in Master Payne's kindness. His very minor curiosity about her existence satisfied, he was already looking past her to the parlor door.

"I think I've heard folk say so about him, yes," he agreed. "He's a good man. He's a good head for business."

Frevisse forced his attention back to her, asking, "You've had many dealings with him?"

"Enough. Yes." Colfoot sidled sideways to pass her, deft on his feet despite his size. "We deal together. Have these ten years past, or more."

Frevisse sidled with him, smiling into his face ruthlessly. "And his wife. She's such a gentlewoman. So kind. She's been the soul of kindness to us, coming as we did all unexpected. Haven't you found her kind?"

Colfoot visibly groped for an answer. Frevisse suspected that so slight a person as Mistress Payne barely impinged on his consciousness. "Yes," he managed, still sidling. "A kind woman. With children, and all," he added, probably hoping that if he added to the conversation, it might end sooner.

Before Frevisse could go on, Master Payne himself opened the parlor door behind her and said with open pleasure, "Will, what brings you here so unlooked for? I thought you meant to be off Burford way by today."

"I did but—" Colfoot's voice had risen but he caught himself long enough to bow to Frevisse and say perfunctorily, "Sister, good day. Your prayers for me." Then he surged past her, his volume mounting again as he declared with mingled anger and satisfaction at Master Payne, "But something out of the way delayed me and I want . . ."

Sure of Nicholas's escape, Frevisse did not care about Colfoot's business, whatever it was. She passed on out of the hall and along the screens passage to the stairs. The waft of dinner smells as she passed the kitchen door reminded her she was behind on her day's prayers if the morning was that far gone. She had meant to follow the Rule today.

"He wants to marry Mistress Dow," Bess said behind her on the stairs.

The surprise of that stopped Frevisse, turning her around

to face the woman as best she could in the narrow space. "He wants to marry Magdalen? Surely she doesn't—"

She stopped herself; Magdalen Dow's life was no concern of hers. But the idea of kind Magdalen tied to Colfoot's rude arrogance . . .

"Oh, no!" Bess shook her head emphatically. "She doesn't. Nor does Master Payne. He thinks she can do better than Master Colfoot if they bide their time."

Frevisse wanted to know more, but not by gossiping with servants. And not cramped on a narrow stairway. She turned away, continuing upward, but Bess chatted on at her back. "When young master goes to London, then likely Master Payne will look for someone for her there. A merchant, very like. Imagine living in London."

Clearly Bess's country imagination was more than ready for a marriage in far and marvelous London. Frevisse wondered what Magdalen's thoughts on the matter were.

A fussy, unfamiliar voice at the head of the stairs interrupted her wondering. "Now, Master Edward, I can't think that your father would want you to. And what has become of Richard I can't . . ."

"Coming," Frevisse said, to warn anyone from starting down, and the voice cut nervously off.

When she reached the top an elderly man in plain priestly black and a tall young man were waiting. No, not a young man. A boy. He was well grown for fifteen, almost his father's height, and had his father's sense of dignity and pride too, to judge by the self-assured bow he quickly made to her, his hand resting on the scholar's scrip at his waist. But for all that he was still a boy, with a boy's long bones and a boy's face untouched yet by much living. And though his gown had the plain cut and color of an Oxford scholar, his belt bore an ornate buckle and its end hung fashionably long almost to the floor.

She smiled at him. "Master Edward," she said, "I hear you are at Oxford. How go your studies there?"

"*Omnia bene,* and I thank you." He cocked an intelligent eye at her. "You are . . ."

"Dame Frevisse of St. Frideswide's priory in the north of the shire."

"Ah, yes. I'd heard everything about you but your name."

Despite the glib reply, Frevisse doubted he had heard very much at all beyond some story that she and Sister Emma had sheltered in his home from the rain yesterday. She looked at the man standing beside him. "You are his tutor, sir? Are you to be congratulated on your pupil?"

"Sir Perys," the man said with a rapid ducking of his head. He was a thin man, not tall, with a habit of clearing his throat before every utterance. "He's a fine boy. A fine young man. An excellent fine scholar."

Frevisse knew she should resist the urge but she did not. Her own Latin was not good, but this was a mere boy. " *'Salvasti de necessitatibus animam meam,'* " she said, hoping she remembered it correctly from the psalter. " *'quoniam respexisti humilitatem meam.'* " You have saved me in my distress, for you have looked with pity on my helplessness.

But Edward was more than equal to the test; lectures and debates at universities were entirely in Latin, and he answered fluently, *"Non opus agere gratiam. Salveris ad domum modestam. Valeant preces tuae voluntam servire quemquam egentem."*

Frevisse held up her hand with an appreciative smile. *"Pace.* My store of Latin doesn't go much beyond my prayers. What I learned else was long ago, and I never had the scholar's knack of it."

Edward smiled and said, " *'Et ne nos inducas in tentationem.'* "

Which was, of course, from the Lord's Prayer: And lead

us not into temptation. Duly chastened and amused, Frevisse replied, "I will know better next time."

Sir Perys tapped Edward on the shoulder with a teacher's proprietary air. "By your leave," he said to Frevisse.

Frevisse inclined her head. With his tutor close on his heels, Master Payne's heir disappeared down the stairs.

Chapter
❧ 9 ❧

FREVISSE WENT ON to Magdalen's room with Bess still behind her. Only Maud and Sister Emma were there. Fever-flushed, Sister Emma was propped up on pillows, fretting at the coverlet with restless fingers while Maud urged her to drink something from a faintly steaming mug.

"I'm hot enough already," Sister Emma complained, the words thick. "I want something cool. There's no use bringing brands to a burning barn."

"But Mistress Dow says . . ." Maud began for what was probably the fifteenth time to judge by her voice's strain.

"Master Colfoot's here," Bess interrupted. "He's come all unexpected and gone in to see the master. Where's she at? He'll be asking to see her surely."

Maud looked around and made a distracted curtsy toward Frevisse. "Gone out." She nodded her head toward the window. "To walk in the orchard for a while, she said, though it's that damp and chill."

The chamber's long window overlooked a pear and apple orchard that a few weeks ago must have been beautiful and fragrant with blossoms. Now it was a canopy of young leaves sloping away to a stream that boundaried the manor from a stretch of forest to the east.

"Should we tell her he's here, do you think?" Bess asked, moving toward the window.

But Sister Emma chose that moment to throw back her covers and swing her feet toward the floor. "I'm *hot*," she declared. "And I want to go home. Where are my clothes?" And they were all three immediately busy in settling her back into bed and persuading her to the medicine that would make her rest whether she wanted it or not.

Nicholas was laughing softly to himself as he slipped out the rear gate of Payne's garden where Cullum had been waiting with the horse they had "borrowed" from Dame Frevisse. If fat Colfoot had a hound's nose, it would be twitching on a hot scent in Payne's parlor right now. But for all he was a dog, the man didn't have a good hound's nose. Nor a fat purse either.

At the memory of last night, Nicholas laughed out loud. As easy a picking as he'd had these past five years. Slip out from behind a hedge, clout the yeoman from behind to send him tumbling into the ditch, and prick a sword into the franklin's fat arse. There'd been no trouble in having the purse handed over and being away without ever being seen. A handsome purse, and a handsome lot of silver in it. And God's teeth, the man had roared afterward, enough to shake the rain off the eaves.

Chuckling, Nicholas jumped into the saddle Cullum had vacated, and took up the reins. "Any trouble?"

"Not here," Cullum said. He took Nicholas's hand and pulled himself up behind the saddle. He nodded toward the stableyard. "But I was talking with Tam in the stable. He was into village this morning."

"And there's talk enough there, I'll wager." Nicholas's grin widened. There was bound to be talk when there was robbery hardly outside the village bounds; it livened the sheep-brained place after years of complacency.

"It's Beatrice," Cullum said.

Nicholas turned in his saddle, finally hearing Cullum's unease. He asked sharply, "What about Beatrice?"

"She was beaten last night."

"Beaten? Who'd beat Beatrice? Why?"

"From what Tam heard, she's not saying. And that's made talk too, 'cause she's bad, Nick. Hasn't left her bed this morning, and Old Nan's talking of sending for the doctor."

Nicholas turned back to face the road. He hated the bother of other people's pain, but Beatrice . . . "We'd best go by way of the village then."

"She's poorly," Old Nan muttered, leading him toward the rattling stairs up to the rooms above her alehouse though she knew he knew the way. "She's that terrified I have to tell her who's coming or she'll set to screaming. I'll just warn it's you and then it will be right."

"Who did it to her?" Nicholas demanded.

Age had shriveled and begun to stoop the alewife, but her tongue still had its vigor. "If she'd tell me, I'd have the hide off him! But she won't say, and I've no way of knowing who comes to see her." Beatrice had her room at the head of the stairs, while Old Nan slept at the back. The downstairs door was left unbarred for just such as might want to come to Beatrice after the alehouse closed; they barred it behind them when they entered and left it unbarred when they left. It was a simple, workable system that allowed Old Nan to say she had no idea if Beatrice ever had a visitor after she had gone to bed herself.

"There had to have been noise," Nicholas prodded.

Old Nan shrugged. "There's often noises; but there's the storeroom between us so I don't hear them. And if I hear them, I don't heed them. There was nothing particular last night. I knew naught till the poor wight came crawling to my door. Wait here," she added as they reached the top of the stairs. She hobbled forward the few steps to tap at Beatrice's slack-hung door. "Bea-girl, it's me, don't fear. I've Nicholas here to see you."

Beatrice made a muffled protest, but Old Nan opened the door anyway, and gestured Nicholas in. "She doesn't want to be seen. Her beauty's behind her, I think, and she knows it. But she's going to have to grow used to it. She'll not earn the pence she once did, that's sure."

Old Nan had done what she could, had washed the blood away and even made herb poultices to lay over the worst of the bruises. But what Nicholas could still see was enough to make him wince; and sympathy did not come readily to him for anyone but himself.

"God's teeth, is it you, Beatrice?"

"Nick?" she whimpered through broken lips. If she saw him at all, it was only dimly; both her eyes were swollen shut by purpled flesh that barely let the tears ooze through. She tried to drag the blanket up to hide herself, but it caught on the raw wood of the bedstead and, lacking the strength to pull it free, she could only lie there with it clutched to her chest.

"Who did this to you?" he demanded.

"Fell," she whispered.

But the bruises on her throat were thumb-shaped, and there were gouges in her wrists and hands where she had been held and fought against the hold.

"You didn't fall. I'm not a fool."

Beatrice moved a hand as if she wished he would hold it, but he could not bring himself to draw nearer. Tears went on seeping from her eyes to run down her ruined cheeks. "Colfoot," she whispered. "Colfoot . . ."

Nicholas came a furious step forward and grabbed her wrist. She shrieked with pain and he let her loose, but leaned over her to ask harshly, "The fat franklin? Why?"

Beatrice was sobbing now, wincing with the pain the

movement cost her. "He'd been robbed. He said . . . Oh, I warned you, Nick!"

Nicholas resisted the desire to take her by the shoulders and shake her. "Why did he come back here? Tell me what he said!"

"He was robbed after he left here. He thought it was someone from here. He'd seen you watching him, remembered you and I . . . that you and I . . ."

"You greasy whore! You told him who I am?"

Beatrice fought to smother the sobs that wracked her body into worse pain. "He described you. Your clothes. Your face. He was sure it was you. He wanted your name."

"And you told him?" Nicholas was standing over her now, wishing she would stop her useless crying. He grabbed the blanket off her so roughly she screamed. "Shut up! Did you tell him?"

"No! No! Not until . . ." Tears and despair won over her attempt to talk. She made a helpless gesture at her uncovered body, as bruised as her face.

"You told him!" Nicholas snarled, flung the blanket at her, and stormed out of the room. He rushed down the stairs and shoved past a blunt-faced youth who shouted something after him as he slammed through the alehouse door.

The pardon was too near to allow a fat fool of a franklin to come in his way to it.

Chapter

⊠10⊠

FREVISSE FOUND THAT Sister Emma now had more reason for her fussing and complaining of discomfort. She was more fevered, and her wrenching cough was painful to watch. She accepted a hot drink almost quietly and barely complained of its bitter taste.

"But my prayers," she croaked as she handed the emptied mug away to one of the waiting-women. "I haven't said any of the offices today. What hour is it?"

"It must be near Sext." Frevisse realized she had missed the prayers for Tierce altogether. Somewhat guiltily she offered, "Do you want to say the office now?"

Sister Emma nodded. "Before I sleep again."

But when she tried to join Frevisse in the opening psalm, she began to cough so heavily that Frevisse had to pause until she had finished. Gently Frevisse held her hand and said, "Just lie quietly and listen while I speak."

Breathless and plainly aching, Sister Emma nodded wordlessly and closed her eyes. *"Ave Maria, gratia plena . . ."* But her evened breathing told when she fell asleep before the office was ended.

Frevisse had nodded for the two waiting-women to withdraw when she began the prayers. Now, finished, she stayed sitting on the bed holding Sister Emma's hand until she was sure the sleep was deep enough to hold her.

Shortly, Frevisse was aware of a door thudding heavily shut somewhere near below her; then of heavy and hurried footsteps and what she thought was Will Colfoot's voice—she raised her head to listen more carefully. The man was declaring angrily about something. His stomping and voice diminished with distance, but now there were other footsteps, lighter, running up the stairs, that brought Frevisse to her feet with the sense of their urgency.

But before she could move away from the bed, Magdalen entered. With something very like panic, she shut the door and leaned against it, breathless both with her haste and her emotion. Her veil and wimple had slipped down around her shoulders, leaving her head bare; she seemed neither to know nor care.

"Magdalen, what's happened?" Frevisse asked, moving toward her, alarmed.

Magdalen stared at her a startled moment, as if she had forgotten she would be there. Then abruptly she drew a deep breath, recovered herself, and straightened away from the door. Pulling her wimple and veil away from her shoulders, she tossed them toward a chest and went to fling herself down in the nearest chair, avoiding Frevisse's gaze. "Nothing," she said. She was still short of breath. "I ran up the stairs, that's all. I—" A knock at the door interrupted her. "Come," she said.

Her nephew Edward entered, followed by another, younger boy who stayed in the doorway behind him. Both looked as if they thought there might be trouble. "Aunt, you were running. Are you well? Has something happened?"

Magdalen drew what she meant to be a steadying breath, but there was a sob in it somewhere. She pushed her hair back from her face. "Will Colfoot still wants to marry me. He was driving his suit over-hard just now. He came on me in the orchard—" She stopped what she had intended to say, but there had been both anger and fear in her voice. "He's gone to speak to your father now."

"He's an oaf!" Edward declared, his face colored with indignation. "I'll tell Father you're upset, and that you want to see him. He should hear more than Colfoot's side of it."

"No, Edward, wait—" Magdalen reached a hand to stop him, but he had pushed past his brother and was gone. Magdalen sank back in the chair, looking abruptly exhausted. "Oh, dear."

The other boy grinned from the doorway, less moved than his brother. "Will Colfoot's more bluster than anything. Father will send him off with a flea in his ear."

"Oh, Richard," Magdalen sighed. With an effort she recalled her good manners and stood up to introduce Frevisse. "Dame Frevisse, this is my nephew Richard Payne. Richard, Dame Frevisse of St. Frideswide's priory."

"Good sir," Frevisse said, giving him a small curtsy.

Richard returned a creditable bow, though its dignity was marred by a wide grin that seemed as much a part of him as his light-brown hair. He was average-grown for twelve years old, with his mother's mild coloring and, Frevisse thought, an easier nature than his older brother.

"Edward just thinks he's older than he is," he explained. "Father is forever having to bring him back to being only fifteen. Ouch!"

Richard spun and dived away into the shadows behind him. There was a scuffle so brief that Magdalen had not time to reach the door before Richard was back, hauling a much smaller boy by the scruff of his tunic. "It's Bartholomew," he said disgustedly to Frevisse. "He wants to meet you too. So he hit me from behind." Someone jerked at the back of his doublet. "And so does Kate," he added.

As he set his unrepentant brother in the doorway, a little girl pushed in beside him. Except that she was slightly taller, they were so alike they could have been twins. Darker-haired than their older brothers, they had their father's and Magdalen's clear gray eyes, bright with a mischief that faded under Frevisse's cool gaze.

"Bartholomew. Kate." Richard lightly thumped each on the head along with their names. "They're all trouble. Don't ask them in."

Frevisse had no particular way with children and did not intend to ask them in. She gave them another slight curtsy. Kate returned it and Bartholomew managed a shy bow and then they both giggled. Frevisse was about to ask them their ages when behind them a girl's voice said, "Here you are. Mother says you're to come. She's in the solar."

"This is my other sister, Katherine," Richard explained. "Now you have to meet her too."

Katherine Payne did indeed resemble her mother, just as Magdalen had said, down to her uncertainty and shy willingness to please. She and Frevisse exchanged curtsies, but clearly her main concerns were to take Kate and Bartholomew to Mother and leave her aunt and guest in peace. With Richard's help, the withdrawal was made somewhat gracefully, and Magdalen closed the door after them.

She had recovered her quietness. A little ruefully she smiled at Frevisse. "Sister Emma is deeply asleep to have slept through all of that."

"Mistress Payne sent some poppy syrup to help her rest."

"That's very good of Iseult. She rarely parts with any. She treasures her poppy syrup for the times when she cannot bear one of her backaches any longer. Though I doubt I've known her to give way to the need above once a year. Isn't it strange?" Magdalen had sat down on the window bench and taken up her embroidery. "Someone who seems so frail, so easily led, isn't actually either. She runs her household very well, and if I suffered with the backache the way I've seen her suffer, I'd have drained that poppy syrup to the dregs at the first chance."

"Did she have a bad fall?" Frevisse asked. She would rather have talked about what had passed between Magdalen and Will Colfoot, but decided to let Magdalen lead the conversation.

"No. Something went wrong at Kate's birth. Iseult's never been fully well since then."

"But she had Bartholomew afterwards."

Magdalen made a sad little shrug. "As will happen," she said gently. "And he's a delightful child. If you don't have to be with him all the day," she added, smiling.

They went on chatting, about the Payne children, about how different it was here from St. Frideswide's, the weather that looked like turning to rain again. Simple things that stirred no deep interest but passed the time. Frevisse asked for some mending to occupy her hands. Bess returned, but Magdalen told her she would not be needed until dinner; Maud did not come at all. Once, distantly, there was more door-thudding somewhere in the house. Momentarily Magdalen was tense again, not looking up but frozen over her work. Then she picked up her sewing and went on as if she had not paused.

Except that she looked out the window unusually often, seemingly watching for something with her work lying idle while she did, she seemed as before. Eventually Frevisse brought the conversation around to Master Payne and found Magdalen had no hesitation at all in talking of him, her respect for her brother clearly deep and strong.

"But he works himself so hard. All this is his doing." She gestured to include the room and all of the house beyond it. "Our father was a freeman and did well enough in his own way. He held almost a hundred virgates under Lord Lovel. But Oliver, beginning with that, has worked his way up to being steward to properties around here for half a dozen lords. They look to him to see that all goes well and to their profit, and it does. There's not a man among all their manor officers he oversees that has any just complaint against him. He's from home too often and that saddens Iseult, but she understands."

How had Oliver Payne become involved with Nicholas then? Frevisse wondered. What business could they share? But that was not a question she could ask. Instead she said, "This Will Colfoot is one of his men?"

"Will Colfoot—" Magdalen began with as near scorn as her soft voice was likely to manage. But she stopped herself, looking again out the window as she said more evenly, "He works for himself and no one else. He began small but now holds lands hereabout, enough to make him feel he's Oliver's equal. No, he feels he's Oliver's better. He feels he's better than most and the equal of everyone else."

"He's not a pleasant man, I gather. And you don't wish to marry him?"

Magdalen shook her head. "He buys lands from freemen who can't go on. He's cruel about it, buying very cheaply from those in the most desperate need and boasting to the countryside about what he's done. He makes money, he manages his properties well, but he's not—a kind man."

Frevisse wondered if Magdalen's husband had been kind. And whether Magdalen valued kindness in a man so much because he had been kind, or because he had not.

"He hopes to be a sheriff someday, I think," Magdalen went on. "And maybe a justice of the peace. And whatever else will give him power and impress men with his greatness. He's very fond of himself." She laughed unexpectedly. "Take care. If he learns you're Master Thomas Chaucer's niece, you'll have no peace from him this side of your convent walls because he'll set out to have you tell your uncle all about him, worthy as he is."

"It's truly sad how my uncle never listens to my opinion

on such worldly matters," Frevisse said drily. "I'd best avoid this Colfoot if I can. Perhaps I can come down with Sister Emma's chill."

Earnest despite Frevisse's teasing, Magdalen said, "Yes. Avoid him if you can."

It was said that there had been a time in the long-past beginnings of the world when there had been three orders of men, each doing in peace the God-given duties they were born to. First were those whose lives were dedicated to prayer, for the sake of their fellow men and all the world. Next were those who fought to protect the godly against the world's evils. Third were those who labored in the fields or crafts, sustaining those who prayed and those who fought for their well-being.

It was a sign of the world's degeneration that this holy division no longer held. A fourth order of men had somehow grown into the perfection of the three: men who neither grew nor made nor prayed beyond the ordinary, nor fought for anything but their own gains. They bought and sold what they had not grown or made, and treated property not as something settled to a family for generations but as another thing for them to buy and sell for no more than the sake of the money it would bring. That their lives were a corruption of God's plan was evidenced by the corruption of their living.

Or so it was claimed.

In the reality of everyday, Frevisse had found neither purity of purpose nor utter corruption in anyone she had encountered, no matter to which of the orders they were supposed to belong. So near as she could tell, the world had degenerated past purity of purpose in anyone, and the most that could be hoped for was godliness enough in whatever life one lived to save one from damnation at the end.

She and her uncle—himself one of the new order of men—had discussed such matters at length upon occasion because, after all, they concerned him very nearly. He lived by what he gained in a variety of ways, had wealth to live whatever life he wanted, and power enough to refuse to serve on the royal council when he chose. He was neither priest nor knight nor simple laborer, and as he once said, "I must have some place in God's plan of things, for nothing happens by chance, only by His will. But if I listen to the priest, I'm very possibly damned for being outside their holy three. What do you think?"

When her uncle asked her what she thought, he always truly wanted to know. He might afterward argue with her, but was always willing for her to argue back. Because of him, Frevisse had come to trust her mind and be bold in using it. That time she had answered, "I think it can be said that none of God's three orders are so pure of purpose now as they were made to be. There are those in every one of them who will not go to Heaven after the lives they've lived on Earth. So if salvation is not assured to those, then I suppose that neither is damnation assured to those outside God's given orders."

Thomas Chaucer had large laughter when he was truly amused, and he had laughed then, reaching out to squeeze her hand. "You glad my mind as surely as you comfort my soul."

This Will Colfoot was also clearly beyond the pale of the three orders; and to judge by everyone's reaction to him—including Frevisse's—he was not among the saved.

But God saw with other eyes than those of man, Frevisse reminded herself. She had no right to judge who was saved and who was damned. That sort of presumption endangered her own soul. And, aware that she had scanted too many services of late, she crossed herself and bent her head in a momentary asking for forgiveness.

Magdalen, gazing out the window, did not notice.

The serving man Jack knocked at the door, come to bid

Magdalen to her brother. She laid her sewing aside with a slight sigh and a tightening of her mouth, but went out silently. Frevisse continued mending the rend in the knee of a boy's hosen.

Sooner than she expected, she heard Magdalen on the stairs, and looked up as she came through the door, then rose to her feet, startled by Magdalen's white, strained face. Not looking at her, Magdalen shut the door and stood with her back against it, breathing rapidly, her mouth set in a hard line. All the color was drained from her cheeks; her gray eyes were huge, glittering. She was in a rage, but there was a tangle of other emotions too that Frevisse could not immediately read—fear perhaps among them.

Frevisse waited while Magdalen visibly recovered herself to the point where she could straighten from the door and say in almost her normal voice, "It seems you're to have my companionship somewhat more sternly than we intended. My brother has asked me to stay in my room as much as may be for the time being."

"Why?" Frevisse asked incredulously. "Because you won't marry Colfoot?"

Magdalen gave a harsh, short laugh and paced toward the window. "No! Oh, no. He doesn't want that either. He will support me in that. He must." She wrung her clasped hands around each other, fighting more inward agony or anger. "No. He's right so far as he understands it. But it will make no difference." She knelt on the window seat and stared out toward the orchard.

"But is he going to keep you here against your will?" Frevisse asked.

"Oliver? No, certainly not." But she did not sound completely certain. "Besides, he has no legal authority over me. I'm of age and widowed, with properties of my own. I can do as I choose." She let go of her anger; misery replaced it in both her suddenly dejected body and her voice. "His only real hold on me lies in our affection for each other, and just now that's making pain enough. I'm not his prisoner, no. I can go. If I want to."

Her tone ended the conversation. Magdalen wanted no comforting, nor did she want to talk of what had happened. In silence she took up her sewing and her waiting at the window. For that was what it was, Frevisse had decided. Magdalen was waiting. For someone? Someone of whom her brother strongly disapproved? Someone certainly not Will Colfoot.

Dinner was brought to them, with a broth for Sister Emma that Frevisse kept warm on the hearth. When she woke, Sister Emma seemed a little better for her sleep, but was still breathing with difficulty and groggy from the poppy syrup. She ate only as much broth as Frevisse had patience to insist on, then slept again.

Mistress Payne came after dinner with her daughter Katherine, as Frevisse finished the prayers for Nones. The resemblance between mother and daughter was even more marked as Katherine, with no childish restlessness, sat demurely with her embroidery—a cushion cover with an intricate pattern that she was working with careful stitches and great patience—while her elders talked past her to each other.

Not that their conversation was very much. Magdalen's confinement was never mentioned, or Master Payne, or Colfoot, only general household matters—that Edward had enough shirts to see him through to winter but that Kate's hems were above her ankles again and there was no more to be let down and what was the point of putting hosen on Bartholomew if he was forever tearing them to pieces with his games.

They had moved on to whether the summer was going to continue as wet as it had been and what would happen to the harvest if it did, when footsteps too heavy for one of the

children and too certain for a servant crossed the room
outside Magdalen's door and someone thudded in loud
hurry on the door. All three women and Katherine looked up
with mingled expressions of alarm.

"Come in," said Magdalen, rising, but was barely to her
feet before her brother had entered.

Without greeting, he said, "Colfoot's been found dead
along the road, hardly a mile from here."

Chapter

11

OLIVER'S GAZE SWEPT all of the women's faces as he spoke. "God's pity on him!" Mistress Payne exclaimed. In unison she and Frevisse crossed themselves, with little Katherine only slightly behind them. Magdalen, her gaze and her brother's locked over something Frevisse could not read, was last. And slowest, her hand tracing the cross across herself as if she barely knew she did.

"What happened to him?" Mistress Payne asked. "Who found him? Where have they taken him?"

"Adam coming back from the farther meadow came on him in the road. There was no help for him, and Adam came back with the news. They're fetching a hurdle now to bring him here. I'm going with them so I can testify to the sheriff when he comes."

Mistress Payne hurried toward the door. "There will be things to be readied. Where will they put him?"

"In the feed room by the stable," Master Payne answered, looking at Magdalen.

And almost as if he willed the words from her, she asked, so low she could barely be heard, "How did he die?"

"Stabbed to the heart." He ignored his wife's pained exclamation. "Or near enough that he must have been dead in minutes. There was not much blood around him, Adam said."

With a distressed sound, Mistress Payne gathered Katherine to her and left the room. Her husband stayed only a moment longer, his eyes locked to his sister's. Then he turned on his heel and followed his wife.

Magdalen sagged down onto the window seat. Frevisse went to her to lay a hand on her shoulder. "What is it?"

Magdalen began to speak, then stopped; began again, shook her head against whatever she had been about to say, and finally managed, "Nothing. He was alive and now, all suddenly, he's dead."

There had been more than that between her and her brother. But Frevisse was not in her confidence and, unable to press Magdalen for more, let it drop and turned instead to the practicalities of the matter.

"The crowner will have to be sent for," she said. "And the sheriff too, for something like this."

Magdalen willingly picked up the shield of conversation. "Surely. My brother will know what to do. He'll see to all of it." She faltered. Before she ducked her head, Frevisse thought tears glimmered in her eyes. Not for Colfoot, surely. Still looking down, Magdalen said, "Will you do me a kindness, Dame Frevisse? A small one?"

"I owe you several great kindnesses, for my sake and Sister Emma's both," Frevisse said readily. "What would you have me do?"

"Go down to supper tonight with the family and tell me afterward everything that was said. About Will Colfoot and . . . anything else."

Frevisse had no trouble making the promise, confessing to herself that it was for more than a service to Magdalen: her own curiosity was among the worldly things she had not yet sufficiently curbed in her nunnery life.

On the heels of her promise, both Bess and Maud

returned. Bess was promptly sent to say that Dame Frevisse would dine with the family tonight, but Maud remained, full of what little was known and eager to talk it around and about for as long as she could make it last. Bess's return let them start all over again. Magdalen did not try to curb them; their chatter filled the time and covered her own silence until they were summoned to fetch Magdalen's supper. As Frevisse went with them from the chamber, she heard Sister Emma's querulous voice from the bed, asking sleepily why there was all this talk. Frevisse did not turn back.

Downstairs in the screens passage, the two women went into the kitchen and she continued to the hall. There the trestle tables had been brought out and set up in U-shape, the opening toward the kitchen end of the hall to make serving easier.

Master Payne was returned from fetching Colfoot's body. He saw her as she entered the hall and came to bring her to the head of the table, where Mistress Payne and Sir Perys were already seated to his right and left. There was an empty place on Mistress Payne's other side where Frevisse presumed Magdalen usually sat; this evening it was to be hers. Master Payne brought her to it; she sat with a low-voiced thanks and turned to wash her hands in the basin of warmed water Edward offered.

He and Richard, as sons of the house, would serve their parents and elders at the head table. It was a gracious custom, and Edward performed it graciously. But when Frevisse, to make conversation, said lightly, "If cleanliness is next to godliness, do you suppose washing could be considered a form of prayer?" he did not make the light, scholarly response she expected, but raised his head as if he had forgotten what he was doing until she spoke. With pity Frevisse realized he must have gone with his father to bring back Colfoot's body and seen violent death for the first time.

"Y-yes," he stammered, clearly not sure to what he was answering. "I suppose so."

Frevisse smiled comfortingly at him as she dried her hands on the towel over his arm.

The three younger children were at the lower table to the right with two women servants sitting with them. On a usual evening, Magdalen's women would undoubtedly have joined them, but tonight would dine with their mistress in her room. Three menservants sat at the leftward table. There would also be a cook and at least one helper in the kitchen, but otherwise all the family was present. Frevisse noted with approval that the Paynes kept a reasonably sized household: enough for their needs but not excessive, and all of them well-kept and quiet-mannered. Even the children Kate and Bartholomew sat quietly here under their father's eye.

They all rose while Sir Perys said grace. His dry, quick voice dealt with all the necessities of the matter briefly, and they sat again to their food.

Inevitably, talk passed with the first platter to Colfoot's death. Frevisse contented herself with listening while she ate. A salad of garden greens was excellent, subtly mixed and seasoned. The sauce for the meat was somewhat thin; Mistress Payne, aware of it, murmured to her under the flow of conversation among the tables, "The flour is running so low, you know, and there's none to be bought around here. We hope for some from London, but our man's not returned yet. And even then—the cost—after last year's harvest . . ."

Frevisse, well aware of how lean last year's harvest had left everyone's stores, and also aware that at St. Frideswide's they rarely had meat from one great holy day to the next, nodded. "It's delicious nonetheless. And I'm sure our cook would love to know what yours has done with the salad. It's quite good."

Mistress Payne flushed a soft pink with pleasure. Her

gentle nature seemed to respond to even the most modest compliment.

But it was the murder and Colfoot that Frevisse wanted most to hear about. It was clear from the general conversation that the man was disliked.

"He's earned many a man's hatred with his ways," one of the menservants said. "The wonder is he wasn't killed before."

"And he kept his ways to the very end," one of the women put in. "They say he beat a woman in the village last night. The one who's at the inn."

The man named Jack made a sound that was the start of a rude comment, but Mistress Payne's glance stopped him short. Another of the men said, "And it was yesterday he was robbed and his yeoman hurt, just outside the village."

"Before or after he beat this woman?" Frevisse asked.

"You, Adam, you were the one was telling us," one of the women said. "Which was it?"

Adam jerked his attention up from his food and looked around as if the answer might be hanging in the air somewhere close. "Before." His blunt face firmed into certainty. "Aye. Before. He'd been at the alehouse . . ."

"Most of the village was," Jack said. "Because of the rain."

"He'd been at the alehouse," Adam repeated, not to be put out of his way. "And he and his man had left and weren't much outside the village when they were attacked."

"From behind," the third manservant said. "Colfoot never saw who 'twas."

"A glimpse of the man's back going into the trees," Adam agreed. "But he must have thought something about it. And after he took his man back into the village for help, once he'd seen him settled in the widow's place for tending, that's when he went for Beatrice."

"He's the one who beat her?" Jack exclaimed. "But not then surely. Not until later, after all'd gone home."

"Aye, when there was none to help her," Adam said bitterly. "When he knew there'd be no one there but her and Old Nan likely—and the door barred if there were so he didn't have to worry about anyone seeing him, he'd just have to wait till anyone left."

He saw their faces and seemed belatedly to realize he had revealed rather much knowledge of Beatrice's ways. He took a sudden interest in his food.

"He beat her near to death, they say," one of the women said. "They say her face—"

"Lovie," Mistress Payne said, questioning rather than ordering, but with a significant look at the children, who were listening avidly. Lovie did not finish what she had been about to say.

Frevisse, with a thought of her own, said, "Colfoot wasn't known for beating women, was he?"

There was general agreement to that; it was folk's purses and hopes he mauled, not their bodies.

"And she wasn't his particular—friend?" Frevisse asked. "He wasn't likely to be jealous over anything?"

"Oh, no." Adam was certain of that. "Nothing of that, I'm sure."

"Then he must have thought she knew something about the robbery," Master Payne said, with the same thought Frevisse had had. "And beat her to make her tell."

Glad of the chance, Frevisse asked, "Did he speak of it when he came to see you this morning?"

"Not about the woman, but about being robbed and his man hurt. He hated for anything of his to be damaged, and worse, to lose anything, particularly money. He came to me because he said he knew now for certain there were outlaws around here, a band of them. He wanted me to join him in demanding the sheriff move against them."

He was very particularly not looking at Frevisse. Matching his neutral tone, Frevisse asked, "What did you say?"

"That I'd had no trouble, nor heard of any trouble lately in the area. That his was surely a single matter, and though surely the sheriff should be told, demanding a great move against outlaws we didn't even know existed seemed unjustified at present."

"And what did he say?" Frevisse asked.

"That I was such a shortsighted fool, it was a wonder anyone trusted property to me." Master Payne smiled with a bitter edge. "He had a temper that matched his arrogance. It was probably that which brought him to beat that woman, if he thought she knew aught."

"Perhaps this Beatrice killed him," Mistress Payne offered. "Or someone who was angry at him for it. If he hurt her so very badly, I mean."

"She's not able to rise from her bed," Adam said.

Lovie put in, "They say her face is ruined."

"But someone else then might have killed Colfoot. To revenge her," Frevisse suggested.

"Who'd revenge a whore?" scoffed the third manservant. "She's no one's particular woman."

"That forester fellow, maybe," said Jack.

Frevisse was aware of Master Payne's sudden, full attention on them. Adam said, "He'd not stick his neck out for her. Only a noddy'd think he would."

"I never said I thought he would," Jack protested.

The third man put in, "But look you, there's a kind of sense to it after all. Why'd Colfoot go after her? Because he thought she knew who robbed him. That'd be the only cause. We don't know what Colfoot knew, but suppose it was her man robbed him and Colfoot figures it out and takes out on her what he can't on old Nick."

"And when old Nick finds out, he goes after Colfoot," Jack agreed. "That's like enough."

Frevisse was suddenly afraid she knew who the forester fellow was; it was unlikely there would be two foresters around with the same name.

Master Payne put in, "Or maybe, by bad luck, it was only theft again and this time Colfoot had time to fight back and died for it. That would be the simplest way of it."

There was general nodding to the possibility. It would surely be more simple if it was a stranger, someone now long gone. But it was not likely, and they all knew that too.

"But whoever did it didn't even take his horse. 'Twas there along the road not fifty yards off, grazing," Jack said.

"A bad thief then, not to take the horse," said the third manservant, grinning.

"Or one who knows horses are easier to identify than coins and didn't want the risk, not after he'd killed the man," said Adam, more thoughtfully.

"And maybe killing was what he wanted all along and not the horse or money at all," concluded Jack.

"Colfoot was well-hated enough by most everyone for that," said Lovie.

Frevisse noticed that now that Colfoot was dead, the hatred was put in the past tense, as if hatred stopped once the man had died. It occurred to her that love went on past death; surely hatred did too. But maybe it was considered less polite to say so. Or less safe, if there was chance of a vengeful ghost hovering near.

"Not hated enough for killing," said the other maidservant.

"Well, he's dead, isn't he? And he didn't fall on his own sword. It was unbloodied."

"But drawn?" asked Frevisse.

"Oh, drawn, surely, lying there in the road beside him," said Adam, remembering. "They didn't even take that."

"They?" Frevisse looked to Master Payne. "Was he attacked by more than one?"

From down the tables one of the men muttered, "Could have been. There's men enough wanted him dead."

But Master Payne said, "There was really no telling. The road is pastern-deep in mud and much used. Everything along that stretch is a mire and no way to read how many might have been there."

"But it's still likely to have been someone from around here," Lovie said. She was clearly fond of the notion they were near to a murderer. "There's been no strangers here or around the village this week and more. Not that anyone's talked about."

She clearly did not count Frevisse as a stranger: she was a nun and well accounted for, not likely to have been out murdering men in the road. But Lovie would gladly hear talk of any others. A pity no one could oblige her, Frevisse thought wryly, and leaned slightly aside to allow Edward to reach past her shoulder to set the last course in front of her: apples sliced and lightly seethed in milk with cinnamon and sugar, a pleasant ending to a well-cooked meal she had not appreciated as fully as it deserved.

For just the moment she was thinking of food rather than the murder. Then Master Payne, in the slow voice of someone just coming to a realization, said, "No. There was a stranger around here today. In the orchard. And Colfoot saw him."

He had all their attentions. They looked at him, and staring into empty air down the hall as if it were from there his thought was coming, Master Payne went on. "My sister was in the orchard this morning alone. A man, a rough stranger, came out of the woods across the stream and spoke to her."

Mistress Payne drew her breath in sharply. Master Payne reached sideways to lay a quieting hand over her own. "Nothing came of it. He offered her no harm. He was only rude. He—presumed to force her into talk with him. Maybe it would have come to more, but it didn't. Colfoot came on them when he went seeking her after he left me."

Lovie put in. "That would be right. He asked me where she was, and I told him—"

A glance from Master Payne silenced her. In the same deliberate voice as before, he said, "Colfoot saw the man had no business being where he was, that he was alarming Mistress Dow. He drove the man off and I doubt he was polite about it. The fellow must have lain in wait for him later and killed him."

"Poor Magdalen!" Mistress Payne exclaimed. "How upset she must have been! No wonder she's keeping to her room. She hid it so well when I was with her. Poor dear. The man must have terrified her."

Frevisse tried to hold her expression blank. Whatever emotions Magdalen had been suffering this afternoon, she had given no sign of terror. Nor had she mentioned any man but Will Colfoot. Whoever the man was that Master Payne claimed was there, if there indeed was one, he was someone more personal to Magdalen than a stranger come out of the woods. Else why would she sit looking for him out the window?

On the back of that thought came another. Where had Nicholas gone when he left Master Payne this morning? To the orchard to meet with Magdalen? And been surprised by Colfoot, who recognized him and returned to the house to tell Master Payne that his sister was meeting with an outlaw?

That would surely account for Magdalen's tension and her brother's present careful choice of words.

And for Will Colfoot's death? Nicholas could depend on Oliver Payne to keep quiet about him, but not Colfoot. Or would Master Payne be desperate enough to protect his association with Nicholas by killing Colfoot himself?

Talk had risen up around Master Payne's idea. It saw

them through to the end of the meal, with no one noting that Frevisse no longer joined in.

But she noticed Mistress Payne was also silent, and suspected her hostess was relieved when Frevisse refused her offer to join the family for the evening, pleading that she should not leave Sister Emma so long to someone else's care. Frevisse washed her hands as Edward held the basin for her again. He was still silent, his eyes down. Even Richard had no glimmer of a smile tonight. No matter how disliked Colfoot had been, he was someone they had known, he had died very near by a violent hand, and his body now lay on the other side of the stable yard, unavoidably in mind.

Rather thankfully, she made her escape upstairs.

As she came to Magdalen's door, she heard Sister Emma's voice. It was thick with her rheum and a little raw but quite determined.

"I'm very sure it's sage that's to be used for rheums. And horehound for my cough. I'm sure that's what Dame Claire always recommends. Not hazelnut. And Dame Claire is very knowledgeable. She has books about these things. She's been Infirmarian at St. Frideswide's for *years*. Dame Frevisse, isn't that so? Didn't Dame Claire use sage and horehound for all of us when we had that dreadful rheum last winter?"

Needing to blow her nose, Sister Emma paused, and Frevisse said quickly while she had the chance, "Dame Claire used sage and horehound, yes. And would have used hazelnut too, but that the wet autumn rotted the nuts before they ripened."

"The Lord gives and the Lord takes away," Sister Emma said philosophically. "So it is sage and horehound, you see," she added to Magdalen standing beside the bed. "But I'll take that if it's all you have." Magdalen gave her the medicine. She drank it and then sank deeper into her covers with a painful breath that ended in a cough. "I'm much better," she assured the room in general. "I just don't seem so yet."

Leaving Maud to draw up the covers and tuck them firmly about Sister Emma, who went on talking while she did, Magdalen came to Frevisse at the other end of the room.

"Is she indeed better?" Frevisse asked.

"She is. The rheum is looser and the cough has gone no deeper. But she won't stop chattering long enough to rest."

"Then she's better," Frevisse said.

Magdalen seemed to forget her patient. In the small privacy that distance afforded them she asked, "And at supper? What was said?"

With great care, trying to keep it all in order, Frevisse told her, even to the gossip of Beatrice and "old Nick," watching Magdalen's response through all of it. But Magdalen, listening intently, showed nothing at all until at the end Frevisse brought out her brother's version of the stranger accosting her in the orchard. Then a slight frown drew between her eyes. Frevisse paused, then asked, "Was he a stranger? Or do you know him?"

Magdalen hesitated a betraying instant, then shook her head, leaving it unclear which question she was answering, or if she were answering at all. Frevisse waited, but Magdalen held to her silence, her eyes on her lap until Frevisse continued. She showed no more emotion until Frevisse finished with, "So now the idea is that this fellow that Colfoot frighted off lay in wait for him and killed him."

At that Magdalen's head jerked up as if whip-struck and, nakedly furious, she cried out, "No! That isn't so! I won't let Oliver do that!" And before Maud or Bess, coming from the other end of the room, could reach her or Frevisse stop her, she had flung from the room, leaving the door wide behind her.

Chapter
12

"Now what was that about?" Sister Emma queried from the bed. "Dame Frevisse, what were you thinking of to do that? You've upset her. It takes both guest and host to make a visit gracious."

Nothing could daunt Sister Emma's Wise Sayings. Distracted, Frevisse went to soothe her with assurances that it was a family matter that had alarmed Mistress Dow, not something she, Frevisse, had done.

"I should hope not!" Sister Emma declared. "What Domina Edith is going to say about this I don't want to think about, and we certainly don't want to make it worse by causing trouble for this family." Frevisse's conscience twitched with the realization that she had never written her second letter. Sister Emma chatted on. "This is a fine house, judging by what little I remember of it and this room, which I gather isn't the best one." Maud and Bess, probably glad to escape their duties to Sister Emma for a while, were the length of the room away. Sister Emma dropped her voice to a whisper to ask, "Who are these people we're staying with?"

Keeping her own voice low, Frevisse answered, "Nicholas brought us here, you remember that. Master Payne is

someone he does business with, and is doing him the favor
of taking us in. They've been very kind to us, Master Payne
and his family. Mistress Dow is his widowed sister.''

"They certainly have all the comforts they could want.
Who is this Master Payne?"

The answer to that took up the little while until darkness
had fully come and Magdalen returned. Frevisse tried to tell
only as much as would content Sister Emma without
rousing other questions. Deliberately she left out anything
about the murder, and as it happened, Sister Emma tired
easily. After some exclamations about what the world was
coming to when a mere steward could rise to live like a
knight—why, her own brother lived hardly so well as
this!—she subsided to a drowse that had deepened to sleep
by the time Magdalen returned.

Clearly, Magdalen was in no better mind than when she
left. To her quick orders, her women brought the truckle
beds out from under the great bed, readying first the room
and then Magdalen and themselves for bed. Magdalen paced
while they did, stood still only long enough to be undressed
and wrapped in her bedrobe, and refused any help with
combing out or braiding her hair. "Let it be," she said
impatiently. "Go away for a while. Or you can go to bed if
you want, Bess, since it's ready. But I don't want to talk or
be bothered. Go away."

Frevisse caught the looks the two waiting women exchanged. Clearly, this was not Magdalen's usual way or
temper. But Maud obediently left, and Bess chose to crawl
into the truckle bed and curl up with whatever thoughts she
had.

Frevisse presumed to go to where Magdalen sat near the
small fire against the evening's damp chill, her hands
clenched into fists. As she sat down across the hearth from
her, Magdalen gave her a sideways glance.

"He holds to that story," she whispered viciously, aware

there were other ears in the room but not able to hold it in. "He says it must have been the man in the orchard. But it *wasn't*!"

"Can you be so sure?" Frevisse asked.

"Yes! He only knew we'd been seen. I don't think he even knew it *was* Colfoot, only that we were seen. He left straightaway."

"What did Colfoot do?"

"He claimed he recognized him. He said he'd seen him in the village last night and knew he was a thief, an outlaw." Magdalen shuddered. "And then he laughed—he had an ugly laugh—and grabbed my arm when I tried to walk away. He said I'd have to marry him now, that Oliver would have no choice. No one else would have me once it was known I met secretly with outlaws. And he would see to it everyone knew."

Frevisse inwardly winced. Nicholas had caused more trouble than he could have guessed by his alehouse carouses and secret wooings. And that was another lie he'd told her; he had said he stayed always in the woods, afraid to be seen by anyone.

Magdalen went on. "Then he made me return to the house with him. I pulled loose when we reached the door and came up here. He went to talk to Oliver."

She stopped, breathless with renewed anger.

"And told him what he'd seen," Frevisse prompted.

"And told him what he'd seen," Magdalen agreed. "And threatened that if Oliver didn't make me marry him, he would defame me through all the countryside with what he'd seen." She looked at Frevisse, her eyes shining with mixed bitterness and anger. "We were in each other's arms, standing there at the edge of the orchard, that's all. Nothing else. But Colfoot meant to say dreadful things and ruin me. When Oliver called me down after Colfoot was gone, he was still furious. Family and reputation mean nearly everything to him."

"But he didn't give in to Colfoot?" Frevisse asked.

Magdalen lifted her head proudly. "He never would! He sent him away, both of them in a rage before they'd finished, but Oliver had made it clear that Colfoot wasn't forcing anyone into marriage. Then Oliver sent for me." The proud head came down again.

"And was equally angry at you."

"Equally. First, because I'd been meeting anyone secretly. And second, because it was someone I should never have been meeting at all. And then that I had let myself be caught, by Colfoot of all people." Her voice broke with the unhappiness of everything. "Oh, Dame Frevisse, I've made so much trouble. I'm in so much trouble."

Without meaning to, Frevisse looked down toward Magdalen's lap.

Laying a hand over her belly, Magdalen said hurriedly, "Not that, no! There's been nothing—that way—between us." Tears glimmered in her eyes but did not fall.

"You'd marry if you could?"

"Instantly. If we could."

"How long have you known him?"

"Nearly a year."

"Meeting always in secret?"

"When we can."

Frevisse sensed more than was said in that, but already had more of Magdalen's confidence than she had ever expected. She reached out, touched her hand, and said, aware it was inadequate, "I need to say Compline now. You'll be in my prayers."

It was more than a way to end their conversation: she had scanted the offices again this afternoon, and felt very much in need of prayer just now.

Magdalen bowed her head. "Prayers are all I can place

my hopes in now. Thank you for letting me ease my heart."

Frevisse had long since concluded that "easing the heart" could be a costly indulgence, but she only said, "I'm sorry I've no help for you."

Magdalen rose to her feet. She looked abruptly very tired, as if letting loose her pent emotions had drained her strength. "I don't think there's help anywhere. It has to be in God's hands. May you sleep well."

"And you also," Frevisse returned.

Chapter

13

FREVISSE, AWAKENING FROM a restless sleep, lay quietly. She remembered where she was and why, and though there was no way to be certain of the hour, she supposed that years of habit had probably roused her for midnight's Matins and Lauds. Under the pressure of the past days, she had missed them. Now would be time to correct that fault; and almost without any effort to recollect them, the prayers began to come to her. For the sake of the others sleeping around her she did not rise, but stayed in the bed with Sister Emma's throaty inhale and exhale beside her and softer breathing from where Magdalen and Bess slept on the truckle beds nearer the floor.

There was comfort in the familiar prayers; they laid a balm over the unease she had taken into sleep with her. But she lacked a prayer book to tell her which psalms were to be said this night. She hesitated, and then simply chose among her favorites. She began them in Latin, but slipped unawares into the English of her uncle's Wyclif Bible, where she had first learned that the psalms in English could be as rich as and, for her, sometimes more comforting than they were in Latin. She finished with a favorite:

" 'The Lord governs me, and no thing shall I lack; in the

place of pasture he has set me. He nourishes me on the water of fulfilling . . . if I shall go in the midst of the shadow of death, I shall not dread evils, for you are with me . . . and my chalice, filled greatly, is full clear . . . Your mercy shall pursue me all the days of my life . . . and I shall dwell in the house of the Lord in the length of days.'"

But when she was done, she was left with only her own thoughts, and the bare fact that she had come to this place and trouble as much by her own doing as anyone else's. And that, having come to it, she must do something. She had solicited pardon for Nicholas, and now it seemed he might be guilty of Colfoot's murder. If he were, he should be hanged instead of pardoned, and she must correct her error.

But after all, he might be innocent of Colfoot's death and wrongly accused. Master Payne had hesitated at supper before revealing a man had been with Magdalen in the orchard. Since the man had almost certainly been Nicholas, Master Payne might well hesitate over accusing him, torn between justice and the peril of putting the hunt out for an outlaw with whom he had undeniably had dealings.

And what if Nicholas were not guilty? It was a shame to ask pardon for a murderer, but greater shame to refuse help to an innocent man. And an unkindness to Magdalen, who deserved at least the truth, one way or the other.

Slowly, regretting her thoughts but unable to avoid them, Frevisse considered whether she could find ways of questioning the Payne household about yesterday. For if Nicholas was not the murderer, then almost surely someone from here was.

But if that was true, then maybe after all any truth she found would be unkind to Magdalen.

Wanly Frevisse wished she were back in St. Frideswide's with nothing but a common day's prayers and duties ahead of her instead of decisions she did not want to make.

*   *   *

Bess went down to morning prayers and breakfast alone, returning afterward with ale and cold meat and bread and a broth for Sister Emma. As she set the tray down, she declared, "I think Sir Perys believes he can hurry the sheriff and crowner on the wings of his prayers alone, and all the sooner if we'll but add our fervor to his own. I thought we'd starve before he'd done. He even prayed for the murderer's repentance as if he thought his words were enough to bring it about." She sniffed. "I'd have to be staring at the rope that was going to hang me ere I'd repent of killing Colfoot."

"Bess," Magdalen said reprovingly. She had been feeding Sister Emma the thin chicken broth, Sister Emma receiving each spoonful like a fledgling bird, with waiting open mouth. Now Sister Emma turned away from the spoon with widened eyes.

"Someone's been killed?" she asked. "Who's Colfoot?"

"A man nobody liked. He died near here yesterday," Frevisse said.

"Someone stabbed him and left him dead in the road almost at our gates," Bess explained. "Ever so many folk hated him, and we don't know who did it."

"There's a murderer somewhere here?" Sister Emma asked with mounting alarm.

"Whoever did this is long on his way," Magdalen said firmly, with a quelling look at Bess.

Bess bent her head, acknowledging the reproof, but went on. "Anyway, the sheriff and crowner can't come too soon for me. And Colfoot's people too, so we can be rid of the body. Even dead, the man's a bother. Jack and Adam and Tam have to keep watch by him turn and turn about all day and night until some of his own folk come to do it. And all the while his murderer is likely lurking near about."

Magdalen's hand spasmed a little; a few drops of soup spilled onto the napkin she held under it before she steadied.

But her voice was calm as she said, putting the spoon into Sister Emma's mouth, "The murderer is surely miles away by now."

Sister Emma swallowed quickly and asked, "Who is the murderer, Dame Frevisse?"

Frevisse's surprise was as great as Magdalen's and Bess's. "I have no idea," she said.

"But of course you do." Sister Emma pouted at her. "You always know those sort of things."

Magdalen turned to Frevisse. "You do?"

Frevisse began to wave such nonsense away, but Sister Emma insisted, "She does it all the time at St. Frideswide's."

"I do not," Frevisse said with some asperity. But Magdalen and Bess went on looking at her, and in defense she added, "Twice things have happened at the priory, and our prioress asked me to find the truth. There was nothing particular about it. All I did was ask questions."

"But she both times proved the crowner wrong. He thought it was someone else and Dame Frevisse showed it wasn't," Sister Emma declared. And opened her mouth for more broth.

"The most lack-witted goose of a girl in Oxfordshire could find the truth out better than our crowner Master Montfort," Frevisse said sharply.

"Well, I certainly had no idea who the murderers were," Sister Emma said. "Nor did anyone else. But she discovered it easily. Old foxes want no tutors, as they say."

Magdalen blinked at this description of Frevisse, then tapped the spoon on the rim of the bowl to rid it of drips and gave it to Sister Emma, and while Sister Emma dealt with it, looked over to Frevisse and asked, "But you are indeed good at finding out the truth of things?"

"Sometimes, with God's help," Frevisse said unwillingly. She had lost much of the pride she might have had in her skill after her failure last Christmastide, when she had been so set on proving one particular person innocent that someone had died who otherwise might have lived.

"Then find out the truth here," said Magdalen quietly.

Frevisse had been enough in Magdalen's company, even this little while, not to be deceived by her quietness. There were passion and strength in her. And in this matter their desires matched; Frevisse wanted the truth as much as Magdalen did. But she also wanted Magdalen to understand the cost. Choosing words carefully, Frevisse said, "I'll need to ask questions. I'll need to know a great deal more than I do about everyone here, both from yesterday and before."

"I'll answer whatever you ask," Magdalen said. "About anyone."

"And if I discover it's someone . . . near to you? Family or . . . friend?"

"Better the truth without than doubt within?" Sister Emma remarked doubtfully.

Magdalen glanced at her, surprised that this wise saying was apt, but then turned her unflinching gaze back to Frevisse. "I'd rather know the truth, whatever the cost."

Frevisse drew a deep breath. She had lost what little appetite she had had for her breakfast, so she folded her hands in her lap and began. "What about your brother?"

Magdalen looked startled. "Oliver? You surely don't think—" She stopped herself and said levelly, "What about him?"

"He's steward to how many lords?"

"Five. He oversees their properties here and in Berkshire."

"And has for a number of years."

"Since before he and Iseult were married. He's done very well."

"And has property of his own?"

"This manor, some lands in Berkshire, some property at

rent in Bedford and Burford and Oxford. All bought at his own cost."

"He's not in debt or other trouble?"

Frevisse watched her response closely, but if Magdalen was aware of anything untoward—such as his league with an outlaw—it did not show in her gentle shrug. "He manages his money well and his investments pay back far more than their expense."

"Has he known Colfoot long or well?"

"They've been acquainted for years, but Oliver has kept distant from him. He's never liked the way Colfoot bullies—bullied—and too often cheated."

"But he wasn't afraid of him?"

Magdalen showed her surprise. "Of Colfoot? Why should he be? Colfoot could never do anything to him."

Until yesterday.

"So there was never a question of your brother forcing you to marry him?"

Bess made a rude, dismissing noise. She had taken Magdalen's place with the bowl of broth and was busily spooning it into Sister Emma's mouth, effectively keeping her quiet. Magdalen smiled slightly. "Oliver could not force me into any such thing. I'm widowed and independent of any man's will that way."

"But he manages your properties?"

"And consults me on his decisions. My husband was somewhat older than I am. He taught me and trusted me to understand as much as he did about what he owned. So I know what Oliver does with what is mine, and why."

"What about Iseult?"

"You mean, does he consult her? Not about their properties, no."

"But he leaves the running of the house and servants to her?"

"Assuredly." Magdalen smiled. "I know she fusses and

dithers, but she's neither foolish nor weak; it's simply her nature to seem so. Oliver by necessity is often gone about his stewardships. Then everything here is in her governing and she does it well. You'll find everything always in order and the servants willing to do all she asks of them because she cares for them nearly as she does for her children. She's fierce about anyone in her care—Oliver, the children, the servants, even me now that I live here."

"What can you tell me about the servants?"

"For that you had best ask Bess. She's among them more than I am."

Sister Emma took the last spoonful of broth, sighed, and settled deeper into the pillows. "I'm sleepy now," she announced, and mopped her running nose. "I really do feel better." She started to cough; when it did not stop Bess came with a basin for her to spit into. "If I could just stop coughing," she said at last. "It does wear me out so."

Magdalen patted her hand. "Coughing clears your lungs. You'll be much better by the morrow."

Sister Emma lay back, murmuring agreement, her eyes closing.

Softly Magdalen said over her head to Frevisse, "I'll stay with her while she falls asleep. Go talk with Bess across the room."

Bess went willingly enough to sit with Frevisse by the farther window. Their heads close together, Frevisse asked, "What was said, at breakfast about the murder and . . . yesterday?"

Bess paused, considering, then answered, "Not anything new, I don't think. And not really that much. The men are tired from taking turns at watch by Colfoot, and I think Mistress Payne has told her women not to chatter, so except for Sir Perys praying, not much was said." She leaned nearer. "I hope it's that stranger that bothered Mistress Dow in the orchard, not someone we know."

Did that mean that Bess was unaware of Magdalen's secret meetings in the orchard? Or was she loyally protecting a secret? Frevisse asked, "Is it true what Mistress Dow said? The servants are happy here?"

"Mistress Payne is a good mistress. And the master leaves much of running the manor to her. Which is as it should be, of course."

"Tell me about everyone."

Bess hesitated. Frevisse prompted, "About Maud? You and she came with Mistress Dow from her old home?"

"We were all she needed, she said. And really she only needed one of us, there's so little to do here, but neither of us had any family to go to so we came with her. I mostly serve her, while Maud is good with her needle and at ironing and does a great deal for Mistress Payne." Bess gave a private smile. "I think she's sweet on Tam of the stables and if Mistress Dow does ever leave here, Maud will find cause to stay."

"Tam?"

"The stableman. Good with the horses, better with the cattle."

"And who are you sweet on?"

Bess blushed a little, very becomingly. "Nobody that notices me," she said shyly. And then added, "Jack."

"So when Mistress Dow leaves, you may stay as well?"

"Indeed I will not." The very idea made Bess indignant. "Jack could just come with me if he had a fancy for me. But he doesn't," she added regretfully. "There's a girl in the village, and if his mother and her parents agree, he'll marry her. Mistress Payne has already said she can work in the kitchen here if she marries him."

"And the other man? Adam, is it?"

"He's a worker, he is. Not that Jack isn't, but Adam seems to want to do even more than he's given." Bess leaned nearer with a knowledgeable nod of her head. "Wants more than is good for him, and I don't mean work either."

Frevisse had never been particularly good at gossip; she had never learned the knack of it. But she knew an opening when it was offered her. She arranged her expression into wide-eyed interest, and Bess nodded again. "Beatrice at the Wheatsheaf. That's the alehouse in the village. Adam goes there more than he ought to, and for more than the ale."

Remembering the talk at supper last night, Frevisse said, "But he's not the only one who wants Beatrice, is he?"

"No, but he's the only one who thinks she's better than she is." Her voice dropped lower, weighty with scandal. "The only one who thinks to marry her."

"He doesn't!" Frevisse did not have to feign her surprise at that.

"He does." Bess was plainly pleased at Frevisse's response. "He's that fond of her that even after her looks have been beaten out of her—did you hear about that?—he still wants her. That's what Lovie says."

"And what of Lovie?"

"She does for Mistress Payne what I do for my lady. Though not so well, though I say it myself. She's more burble than brains. . . ."

Bess had very clear views about everyone in the Payne household. Carefully Frevisse gleaned all that she could, right down to the boy who helped Tam in the stables. "He's Lovie's brother. Not very bright but a hard worker," Bess confided.

When Sister Emma was soundly asleep, Magdalen joined them and added her comments. By the time they had finished, Frevisse felt she could now move knowledgeably through the household, to see what else she could learn.

"The younger children will be at their lessons with Sir Perys this time of the morning," Magdalen said. "And Edward and Richard with their father since he's home. He'd meant to be off on another of his circuits today and be gone likely a week, but with all this he's had to stay."

"Mistress Payne?"

"Anywhere, depending on where she's needed. Try her bedroom across the way as the children will be in the solar at their lessons."

Before going out, Frevisse made sure her veil was on evenly and pinned firmly in place, not so much for the sake of appearances but to give herself time to brace for her intrusion into the Payne household. There was need for her to do it—and reasons why she should not—but she felt committed to it now.

At her knock on the door across the way, someone bid her enter, and she found herself in the house's great bedroom. Like Magdalen's chamber, it went the full width of the house, was open to the rafters, and had a fireplace in one wall. But it was altogether a larger room, with not only the wide bed that Master and Mistress Payne shared, but two other beds where their younger children slept and an upright loom in a farther corner. As with Magdalen's room, there were chests for storage and clothing, and various stools and a chair, but the long window in the wall opposite the fireplace overlooked the foreyard and the fields beyond the road rather than the orchard. The servant woman Lovie was seated there, where the overcast morning's light was best, with a pile of linens beside her.

She was glad Frevisse was come. She would have been glad of any company, but someone new to talk to was best of all. At her eager invitation, Frevisse sat down and, despite Lovie claiming she did not need help, began to fold linens with her.

"Everything is all upset with this death," Lovie said. "Your visiting was exciting enough, you going astray in the woods and Sister Emma—that's her name, isn't it?—falling ill—it's bad weather for traveling, I can't help but say—and how fortunate you fell in with that forester fellow who thought to bring you here."

Frevisse agreed readily to all of that, and asked, "Do you see much of him around here?"

"Now and again. He's best acquainted with Master Payne and sometimes comes but not often, no."

"He's better known in the village, I gather."

"Oh, I think so. At least some places in the village."

Lovie gave a knowing smile and wink that invited further questions. Frevisse, choosing not to feign innocence, said, "And Beatrice at the Wheatsheaf prefers him to Adam?"

Lovie made a little, scandalized sound. "How talk does fly around! People will say anything to anyone." But then she nodded and leaned toward Frevisse, her voice lowered over what was certainly no secret. "But I think Adam may have a better time of it now. Old Nick won't want her now she's lost her pretty face."

"But Adam will? In spite of that and . . . and . . ."

Lovie saved her the trouble of finding a polite word by nodding vigorously. "Oh, Adam knows all about her and has liked her anyway, right along. Still does, even after seeing her yesterday."

"He saw her yesterday?"

"He did indeed. As soon as he'd heard of it, he was off to the village. Was there straight after old Nick saw her, and no comfort she'd had from him either, I guess, from the way Adam told it. He was that mad at old Nick as much as at Colfoot after he'd talked to her. No, she'll be more willing to listen to Adam after this. She's not likely to have anyone else, from what they say about her face. It's just as well Colfoot is dead, so far as Adam is concerned. He was angry fit to kill him yesterday." She popped a dimpled hand over her pretty mouth. "Oh, I don't suppose I ought to say that, things being as they are." But she sounded more amused than worried that Frevisse might take her seriously. She picked up another towel to fold. "Only I surely shouldn't like to be old Nick next time Adam comes on him. No, I wouldn't."

Overwhelmed by such a flood in return for her little question, Frevisse held quiet a moment. A random spatter of rain passed across the window. Lovie sighed. "I do believe this is going to go on forever. The laundry always smells smokey now, from drying in the kitchen."

From beyond a door opposite where Frevisse had entered children's voices rose in a concerted murmur that told they were repeating lessons. Frevisse nodded toward them. "Sir Perys surely earns his keep here, teaching all the children."

Lovie giggled. "He'd no great problem with the older boys, and little Katherine is at least biddable, but I'd not try teaching that Bartholomew for all the gold in Oxford, and Kate's no better."

Beyond the door something heavy thumped to the floor and Bartholomew's young voice yelled, "I won't! I don't want to!"

There was the smack of a rod and a yelp. Quiet returned. Lovie covered another giggle. "He's a high-stomached man, is Sir Perys. He doesn't take arguing from anyone he thinks under him. And he thinks most anyone is under him if they're not an Oxford scholar, even if they are paying his wages."

There was the sound of footsteps on the stairs. Frevisse went on folding the last of the linen, finishing as Mistress Payne entered with Maud behind her. Frevisse and Lovie rose to their feet respectfully. Mistress Payne fluttered her hands at them from under an armful of dusty-pink cloth, yards of wool as finely woven as it was beautifully dyed. Cut threads hanging from the empty loom in the corner indicated where it had been made, and after Mistress Payne's flustered greetings and her own explanation that she was simply tired of being in Magdalen's room and had been passing the time in talk with Lovie, Frevisse complimented her on the cloth that Maud was now spreading out on the bed. "What are you planning to make?"

"I had thought gowns for the girls. But then again I've thought of a cloak for myself. But I don't know."

"Your old cloak is patched in three places along the hem, mistress," Lovie said. "It's going to be a disgrace for you to wear it by next winter. Your girls have winter gowns enough for the while."

"Yes, I suppose." Mistress Payne was not convinced, though her hand lingered lovingly over the fabric. "But I doubt there's enough here for a cloak after all."

"There is if we turn this the short way," Maud began. She swept the fabric off the bed and around Mistress Payne's shoulders, keeping it in place with one hand while holding a length of it out to the side. "See now, this would work well. We cut this long end off and make a hood of it, and then cut the center out in triangle shape, turn it upside down and sew the pieces together, making a bell-shaped cloak that would be perfect."

"And the color is beautiful on you," Frevisse added.

Mistress Payne blushed a soft rose color that nearly matched the wool. She murmured something about Frevisse being kind. Frevisse murmured politeness back, then asked, "But is there anything I can do besides simply sitting? Some"—she glanced at a workbasket beside one of the chairs—"mending perhaps?"

Mistress Payne followed her glance, and sighed the weary sigh of a mother who cannot keep up with her children. "This tunic of Bartholomew's," she said, picking it up from the basket. "He's torn it again. Do you think . . . ?"

She held it out doubtfully. The tear was jagged and almost a hand's-length.

"I am not skilled at invisible mending," Frevisse warned. All the world coveted the needlework of English nunneries, but none of it came from Frevisse's fingers. Her talents lay elsewhere.

Mistress Payne laughed; it was a surprisingly merry sound. She said, "Neatness is wasted on Bartholomew. He'll have the edges apart again before anyone notices how well or poorly they are joined."

While Maud spread the cloth out again and set to cutting, and Lovie left with her pile of folded linen, Frevisse and Mistress Payne sat down to the mending. The brief shower had passed; sunlight made fickle play among the clouds, and sent random beams through the windows. Mistress Payne sorted through her skeins of thread, and passed one to Frevisse that most nearly matched Bartholomew's blue tunic.

"Not that matching colors matters either," she said. "He usually has his clothing covered in dirt very soon after putting them on. But one feels obliged to try."

"Were all your sons so lively when they were young?"

"None of them so lively as Bartholomew, I must needs say." Mistress Payne's customary fluttering uncertainty was replaced by pleasure when she spoke of her children. "Edmund was nearest. He was the eldest and we meant him to follow his father, but I think he would eventually have gone a-soldiering instead. He could never hear enough of the French war. He had the heart of a lion. He loved adventuring. Just like Bartholomew." Her face shone for a moment with deeply remembered affection; then her smile quavered and she blinked rapidly and bent over her sewing. "But one can't always win against fevers. And now Edward is our eldest."

To help her move away from memory of her loss, Frevisse said, "He seems quite scholarly. Magdalen tells me he's to be a lawyer."

"Indeed, yes. None of the others have his bent for learning. And he loves it. I thought for a while he might enter the Church, but he says he has no time for playing churchmen's games, for mocking God with pretended prayers while living a worldly life." Mistress Payne suddenly realized who she was talking to. "Oh! Your pardon, please!"

Frevisse smiled reassuringly, with honest amusement. "No pardon is needed for your son's very accurate observation of all too many churchmen."

Mistress Payne gave her a friendly, puzzled little frown. "You're far easier to talk with than I . . ." She blushed again, ducked lower over her sewing, and said hastily, "Yes, Edward is very good with words. Not that he isn't brave, mind you. He and Edmund used to have terrible fights and neither of them would back off a step. Sir Perys used to have to beat them apart with his rod. I did hate that. Thank goodness Richard is a more peaceable sort. Nothing puts him in a temper. Or almost nothing. Richard will follow his father and become a steward. He has a good head for that, though not at all for scholarship."

Led on by Frevisse's questions, Mistress Payne chatted on happily about her children and her household. Some of it Frevisse had already learned from Magdalen or Bess or Lovie; most seemed of very little use, and when she had finished with the tunic she was thinking how to go about her business elsewhere when Mistress Payne said, "So even with times so hard this year, we can't think of turning out any of our people. They're loyal to us and we are to them. And of course we try to help all we can, even if they're not of the household. Just yesterday, I rode out to the Wilcox cottage to see if there was anything I could do for the mother. She's down with a flux. I meant to send one of the women with soup, but decided I should go myself." Mistress Payne shook her head sadly. "I fear it's going to be the worst for her."

Keeping her voice even, Frevisse asked, "When did you go?"

"Yesterday."

"Before or after dinner?"

"Why, just after—" Mistress Payne broke off, her face a confusion of expressions. "Why, just after Master Colfoot was here," she said, more slowly than she had begun. "Oliver was so angered I thought I would go then and everything would be settled when I returned. I must have been at the Wilcox cottage when Master Colfoot was— killed."

She looked as pale as if she had witnessed the murder herself. Frevisse knew that for kindness's sake she should change the subject, but she said instead, "Did you go alone?"

"Oh, no, of course not." It was improper, as well as dangerous, for a woman to travel the roads unescorted; Iseult was vaguely surprised that Frevisse felt a need to ask such a question. "Jack went with me. I wanted Adam, because he's bigger and bolder, but he was gone somewhere. Isn't it just dreadful when something like this happens? We loathed the man, and even now none are truly sorry he's dead. I just wish the sheriff would hurry and come, so his people can take him away from our holding."

"I heard the men say they doubt the sheriff and crowner will be here before tomorrow," Maud put in.

"Oh, no!" Mistress Payne exclaimed. And that set off a discussion of royal officials, who were underfoot when you wished they were three shires away and never to hand when you wanted them. Since this was not to her point, Frevisse made her excuses and went away.

Chapter

🌿14🌿

Alone for a few moments on the stairs, Frevisse paused to consider. Judging by the number of people who seemed to have hated Colfoot, the main question of who wanted him dead had too many answers, but for just here and now, who were the possibilities? Master Payne perhaps, because Colfoot had threatened him through Magdalen. And because he had a temper that was feared even by his wife. Magdalen herself, in fear of Colfoot's threat to marry or ruin her. And most clearly, Nicholas because Colfoot had come between him and Magdalen and was a danger to his pardon. How much would her cousin dare to win his pardon, she wondered. Or Adam, in revenge for what Colfoot had done to Beatrice.

She closed her eyes in contemplation. Magdalen must be innocent; she had been in her room, had had no chance to strike at Colfoot. Unless she had asked someone else to do it. If so, it would have had to have been when she returned to the house, between pulling free from Colfoot and entering her room; or else while she was on her way to her brother or returning from him when he first summoned her after Colfoot had left. Who could she have asked? One of the serving men surely. Probably Adam or Jack, since Tam was usually in the barn. But possibly Tam, if he had happened to be where she could speak to him.

Frevisse could not find any of that very likely, but there were other reasons for learning where each of the men had been. Magdalen was not the only one who could have asked them to kill Colfoot; Master Payne was much more likely and would have had more chance to speak to them, and maybe they were loyal enough to the family to do as he asked.

So she also needed to know where he had been after Colfoot had left. And did he merely have knowledge of or did he help in Nicholas's extortions? Or was Nicholas extorting from *him*? And how many others in the Payne household knew what Nicholas actually was?

She would also greatly like to know where Nicholas had gone after he left Magdalen in the orchard. Had he waited close by for some word from her? If he had, Magdalen could have sent one of her women to tell him. Bess had been in the room all afternoon, hadn't she? But not Maud. Warned by Maud, or some other of the women, Nicholas could have gone after Colfoot and killed him, for his own sake as well as Magdalen's. Why had Magdalen been looking out the window all yesterday afternoon, if not for some sign from her lover?

But there was no way short of talking to Nicholas to find most of that out. And no chance of talking to him. The best she could hope for was to find out where Maud had been. But Maud was still with Mistress Payne, so that would have to wait.

She considered searching out Master Payne then, to ask him directly about his relationship with Nicholas. But she suspected he would not approve of her interest or her questions. So maybe she had best wait to speak with Master Payne until she had finished with everyone else. She went on down the stairs and into the kitchen.

It was a long room, with a wide fireplace and a bake oven built into one end wall, shelved aumbries, their doors weighty with locks, and two massive worktables down its center. Various bundles of herbs and onions hung from the rafters, and the whole room was warm with cooking heat and dinner smells. The cook and his kitchen boy were at the farther table, the boy grinding something in a mortar, the cook brooding over his shoulder as if it were gold they were assaying. Neither even glanced up at her.

But as she had hoped, given the drizzling day and the fact that she had seen them nowhere else around the house, Mistress Payne's other maidservant and Jack and Adam were gathered around the nearer table. There was always something anyone could turn their hand to in a kitchen as an excuse to be warm and in company, and they were all justifiably busy. Jack was washing rhubarb that, judging by its fresh mud and his damp feet, had just been brought in from the garden. The maidservant was unleafing and slicing it into small bits in a large bowl. Adam was sitting with a whetstone, sharpening an array of kitchen knives laid out on the table beside him.

They all looked up and acknowledged her coming, Adam starting to rise to his feet respectfully. But Frevisse waved him back down.

"I'm simply weary of keeping to Mistress Dow's chamber, and Mistress Payne is busy so I thought I'd see if there were company and talk here," she said with disarming friendliness.

"Oh, aye, here's good company," Jack said cheerfully. "Better than being out in the rain anyways."

Both he and the maidservant seemed in good humor. They chatted with her easily about her journeying and the other nun's health, and in low voices were mildly rude about the cook, claiming that he never thought of aught but food and if he had the means, he'd be as wide as his own kitchen.

"But it never looks good to a master to have too fat a cook—it means the cook is eating more and better than he is," Jack said. "I'd have been a cook if my family could have apprenticed me anywhere."

"You'd not," the maidservant protested. "What would you want to do that for?"

"Why would I want to be warm and dry and with all I want to eat? Occasionally greasy and yelled at maybe, but I'm yelled at anyway. And mud's as bad as grease." He gestured at his boots. He had tried to wipe them off, but they were still well along to be being ruined with old mud as well as new. "Just try in this weather to keep them clean," he grumbled. "Yesterday I'd just come back with Mistress Payne and cleaned them off, and had to turn around to go fetch bastard Colfoot's body—asking your pardon, my lady—and mire myself to the knees again. Pity he couldn't have found a drier place to die."

"You're not the only one," Adam said. He had hardly spoken. The steady whet-wheet of his knives sharpening had made a background to their talk. Now he spoke bitterly. "And you're not the one who's had to clean not only your own but Master Payne's and young master's boots as well."

"You'd not have had to clean yours so much if you'd not gone off daft to the village in the morning and put yourself in such a stomping temper," Jack returned. "And for a broken-nosed whore at that. Begging your pardon, my lady," he added as Adam rose up from his chair with clenched fists and reddening face.

"Mind your tongue about Beatrice!" he growled.

"How does she?" Frevisse interposed. "I heard she was fearfully hurt."

Adam fought between his anger at Jack and the need to give her a civil reply. Civility and his desire to talk of Beatrice won. He rubbed a rough hand over his blunt face and sent a last glare at Jack. "She looks worse than she is,

Old Nan hopes. We thought maybe she was broken inside as well as battered all over her face and ribs, but seems not. She's hurting less today anyway."

"You were there again this morning?" the maidservant asked disbelievingly.

Adam cast her a warning look. "I had to know. No one else but me and Old Nan care a farthing for her."

"And she's doing better?" Frevisse prompted.

"We think so. The bruises look fearful but the cuts are likely to heal clean. Only . . ." He was caught between the need to talk about her and the pain of what he had seen. "Only he did things to her that aren't going to mend back to where she was."

"They say her beauty's gone," the maidservant said gently.

Adam bent over whetstone and knife again. "Her looks won't be what they were. But she'll still be Beatrice."

Frevisse saw Jack's face twist toward a rude comment before he thought better of it. Adam looked up at her across the table. "She's had a bad life, my lady, but her heart is good. She's been as good as life would let her. Now, if she'll let me, I'll make it better for her."

Jack could not hold himself in one that one. "You dafter! You haven't gone and promised her anything, have you?"

Adam's heavy features thickened with sullen stubbornness. "We talked yesterday. She was all tears after that forester fellow left her. Much he cares. He browbeat her into telling who'd done it to her, and then went off in a rage without so much as a kind word to her. But I listened to her, and then she listened to me. Right through to dinnertime I sat with her. And I'm glad Colfoot's killed or I'd have to do it myself. But he's maybe done a good turn in his life after all, not meaning to." He transferred his glare from his work to Jack and said, "So at least I came by my morning mud honestly. You rode with Mistress Payne and had no business being mired past the ankles the way you were when you came home.''

"Here now," Jack exclaimed, slapping down a wet rhubarb stalk on the tabletop. "You think I spent my time kicking my heels in the doorway there? The place stank of bowels—God save the woman—" He crossed himself. So did Frevisse and the others; the flux could kill as quickly as fevers did. "—so I went off to see if the rain had drowned out the winter wheat in Over Field yet."

"Has it?" the maidservant asked. How well they ate next winter would depend on how well the crops grew.

"Not yet. But we'd better have some dry weather soon, and for longer than two days at a stretch."

"Which way is that from here?" Frevisse asked casually.

"Go to the village and turn right between Tompson's and Lame Bet's, south on that track you come to Wilcox's. Over Field's beyond there a way."

No one seemed to wonder why she asked. Frevisse had long since noticed that most folk felt what interested them surely should interest everyone else. "Opposite the way Colfoot went and was killed," she said.

"Not really so far," Jack said. "The way the track curves around, you could cut across only two fields from Over Field and be on the road he took."

He said it with such openness that it would have been difficult to believe he had crossed those fields, met Colfoot, killed him, and crossed back; some shade of guilt should have had in his answer. And the timing seemed wrong; if he had ridden with Mistress Payne before following after Colfoot, Colfoot would have been further along the road from the manor than Frevisse had the impression he had been. But perhaps she should have something better than an impression.

"You both went to fetch Colfoot's body?" she asked.

Jack and Adam nodded together. "Us and Master Payne.

We took a hurdle and a horse and hauled it home," Adam said. "And it wasn't easy, with the mud and him no bird-weight. Grown fat on other people's famine, may he be sizzling in Hell."

"It was a half mile or more. That must have been hard indeed, wasn't it?" Frevisse asked.

"Hard enough but, nay, not nearly so far. A quarter mile maybe," Adam said.

"It was you found him dead, wasn't it?"

Adam laid the knife he was now sharpening a little harder against the whetstone. His tone was grim with things he did not want to remember as he answered, "Aye. Lying there like a bled pig. A big lump in the road."

"There was much blood?" the maidservant asked with fascinated horror.

"Not so much," Adam granted grudgingly. "It was mostly a great smear on his gown."

"And you didn't see anyone?" Frevisse asked.

"Nobody at all. But I was coming from the manor. Whoever did it would have been headed t'other way, I'd guess, away from the place. They'd not be daft enough to stand about gabbing once they'd done it."

With a sudden thought concerning time, Frevisse said, "You were going to check a pasture when you found him, I think you said. But you'd been to the village first, seeing Beatrice. Did you come back here and then go on to the pasture, or right from the village?"

Adam gave her a suspicious look from under his brows before answering grudgingly, "Nay, I went straight from the village, not stopping here. I was supposed to see to the pasture and thought I'd best do it before I came back, behindhand as I was with going to see Beatrice."

"And saw no one on the road between the village and Colfoot's body?" Frevisse asked, to allay the suspicion he was clearly beginning to form about her questions.

"Saw nobody until I saw Colfoot. Anybody who'd done it wouldn't be larking along the road. They'd be off behind the hedges or into the woods. Came that way too, and was lying in wait for Colfoot, is what we've guessed."

The maidservant shivered. "It was someone as meant to kill him, not just finding a chance but coming after him from somewhere else. That's what Master Payne says. It wasn't anyone from here, killing him on our own doorstep nearly."

"Could it have been outlaws maybe?" Frevisse suggested. "Aren't there outlaws around here?"

Glances passed among the three servants before Jack answered. "If there are, they've made no trouble in a while and a while."

"They haven't?" Frevisse said with strong surprise. "That seems odd for outlaws."

Jack laid a finger aside of his nose to show there was something near enough to smell but that he was too wise to mention it.

Adam was feeling less discreet. "Well, someone robbed old Colfoot, didn't they? He didn't break his own yeoman's skull and cut his own purse the other day."

"Knowing old Colfoot, I'd not put it past him if it meant some sort of profit down the way," Jack answered.

"And you're probably going to claim he stabbed himself too," Adam mocked.

"Oh, aye," Jack returned. "He maybe found he'd cheated himself over something and was so ired he killed himself in revenge."

"Likely it was the fellow bothering Mistress Dow in the orchard who did it," the maidservant said soothingly. "A stranger and long gone. That's who it surely was."

The talk began circling over the same ground, so Frevisse excused herself. Adam at least had begun to be suspicious of her questions, so she had better leave them for a while. She sought Master Payne, but he was not in the parlor. Overhead in the solar she could hear lessons ending, Sir Perys loudly directing the children to put their slates away and be careful while they did it, so she retreated across the hall, having no desire to be caught in the flood of children she heard starting down the stairs from the solar to the parlor.

She momentarily considered going out to the barn to talk with Tam, but decided she should return to Magdalen's room. On the stairs she met Maud. Maud stood aside in the narrow space to let her pass, but Frevisse paused and said conversationally, "That wool will make a beautiful cloak for Mistress Payne. Mistress Dow says you're an excellent seamstress."

Maud smiled, pleased. "I do seem to have a hand for it."

"You don't mind serving both women at once? Doesn't it become burdensome for you?"

"Oh, no, never at all. They're both kind beyond words. And there's little Mistress Dow needs me for these days."

"Everyone is talking about the murder," Frevisse said. "Everyone seems to remember where they were when it happened. I think I must have been feeding Sister Emma broth. Isn't it odd to think of doing something so ordinary"—she had no idea at all what she had been doing—"when someone was dying just down the road?"

Warmed to conversation by talk of her two ladies, Maud said readily, "Haven't I thought of that too? I was measuring little Kate for a new gown in the solar when it must have happened. Something I've done so often, and now every time I do it again, I'll think of Master Colfoot being killed. Isn't it sad?"

Frevisse agreed. "Does Kate stand still for being measured?"

"Not her!" Maud laughed. "I was just persuading her to it when we heard the shouting in the hall that was Master Colfoot come to argue with Master Payne. Then I had a job of it to keep her from slipping down the stairs to listen at the parlor door after they went in there! She wouldn't stand still and pay heed until they'd finished."

"Could you really hear what they were saying?" Frevisse asked with encouraging awe.

Maud made a disgruntled face. "No. I could hear they were angry, but they kept their voices too low for us to hear the words. And don't think Kate didn't try. But they remembered walls can have ears and we didn't hear a thing. But I didn't finish measuring the child until they'd finished, she wouldn't heed me until then. She can be a little beast." But Maud said it fondly, smiling, and Frevisse smiled with her and went on up the stairs.

So Maud had been busy with Kate and could not have spoken to Magdalen when Magdalen was going to her brother. Frevisse had the weary feeling she had learned a great deal that morning, and solved nothing.

And then at the top of the stairs she saw Sir Perys bowing his way out of the Paynes' bedroom. She waited while he closed the door and, when he turned around, curtsied to him with a pleasant smile. "Were you reporting to Mistress Payne on how your young scholars are doing?"

"The only scholar in the household is Master Edward," he answered tiredly. "The others learn what little they learn only when pressed to it by my rod."

He looked as much harassed as fatigued, and Frevisse reflected that his lot might well be the hardest in the household. He was both cleric and tutor, with probably small time for his religious devotions and much time given over to pupils who wanted none of his teaching. But as she started to say something encouraging, Edward pushed back the curtain that closed off the room he shared with Richard and said, "Sir Perys?" He was dressed plainly in a dark blue gown of modest cut, belted with an ordinary black belt. He bowed to Frevisse, but before he could speak, Sir Perys took

the open book Edward had in his hands and peered
nearsightedly at the page.

"You want help with this? This is not difficult!" He read
in rapid, fluent Latin, "*'Improperium exspectavit cor meum
et miseriam, et sustinui qui simul mecum contristaretur, et
non fuit; consolantem me quaesivi, et non inveni.'* There's a
fine text for you, I must say. Very appropriate for me as
well!" He gave the book back. "Foolish boy!"

Frevisse read and spoke both English and French with
ease, but though her Latin was slight, yet this sounded
familiar. One of the psalms, she thought.

Edward was looking at her, embarrassed, apparently, to
be scolded in front of her. "I—I beg your pardon, my lady,"
he stammered. "I would not—"

"Edward, dear, are you still at your studies?" It was
Mistress Payne, standing in her bedroom doorway, concern
on her face and in her voice. "Shouldn't you do something
else for a while?"

Before Edward could answer, Sir Perys said officiously,
"Now, I pray you, my lady, trust me in this."

"But he looks so tired."

"If he's tired, it's from being hither and yon all the time,
wearing himself out at fruitless pastimes."

Mistress Payne came to feel Edward's forehead. "You're
not fevered are you, dear?"

"I'm very well," Edward said, pulling himself away. "I'm
not tired. I'm quite well."

He was taller than his mother by almost a full head. It was
amusing to see her worrying up at him like a hen whose
chick had overgrown her. He caught her hand and kissed it,
summoning a smile. "Mother, how can I become the first
scholar in England and a lawyer to make you all proud if I
don't work hard?"

She looked back to Sir Perys. "But you will be careful not

to over-burden him? Must he study as hard at home as he does in Oxford?"

Sir Perys huffed up. "I am quite capable of judging his needs in this. I assure you, my lady—"

Frevisse, with the impression that this was a well-worn matter among mother, tutor, and son, retreated to Magdalen's room.

Chapter
◈ 15 ◈

FREVISSE FOUND THAT Magdalen's room looked almost like
sanctuary to her after having to deal with so many people in
so short a while.

Unfortunately, Sister Emma was wide awake, propped up
on pillows and trying to chatter around the impositions of
her cough. It had worsened again, but she was endeavoring
to ignore it for the sake of bright conversation with Bess
beside the bed and Magdalen sitting again on the window
seat where the light was best for her embroidery.

"Yes, you should see my brother's place. Not so new as
this, of course. Well, of course not; our family has been
there for *generations*."

Three, Frevisse happened to know; a grandfather had
made his fortune out of plunder in the French war and
bought property to go with his new-made knighthood.

"But very pleasant. My room when I was a child was so
large and all my very own. After my sisters married and left,
of course. Or it seemed very large to me then. I was scarcely
more than a child when I entered the nunnery; my faith
came to me *very* young and I've never regretted—"

Sister Emma's father, having spent most of his father's
riches without making any of his own, had found the

dowering of his third daughter into a nunnery cheaper than a marriage settlement.

Frevisse caught herself short on that uncharitable thought, and for penance went to succour Bess.

Sister Emma was delighted to see her. "Dame Frevisse," she began, "we've been having such a talk!"

By the glaze in Bess's eyes, Frevisse could imagine who had been talking. But Sister Emma's enthusiasm was cut off by a spasm of coughing, and Frevisse picked up a goblet from the table and held it for her while she drank. Taking it back from her, she surreptitiously felt her hand. It was still hot.

Subdued and flushed, Sister Emma sank back into the pillows. "That does take the strength right out of me," she sighed. "The spirit is willing but the flesh is weak, you know. Now what was I saying? What have you learned about this murder?"

Magdalen stood up abruptly, dropping her embroidery in a careless heap on the window seat. "I'm going out to walk for a while. I've been in too long."

"Mistress, your brother said—" Bess began.

"My brother is not my master! I'm going no farther than the orchard," Magdalen answered, and left.

Frevisse and Beth exchanged sympathetic glances with each other, and then, in mutual comprehension, looked at Sister Emma, who stared with unblemished surprise at the door. "My goodness," she said. "Such haste makes waste, I've always said. But about the murder, Dame Frevisse. I've been thinking . . ."

They let her talk on, with the hope she would exhaust herself and sleep again. But whenever she seemed easing toward drowse, another spasm of coughing would bring her fully awake and talking again.

Frevisse was beginning to think she would fall asleep before Sister Emma would, from sheer tedium, when the afternoon's quiet was pierced by a scream that rose and broke from somewhere outside, followed by a shout and then more shouting, now from the manor yard itself.

"Lord have mercy!" Sister Emma exclaimed. "What—?"

Frevisse was already to the door and out. Reaching the stairs ahead of Edward, Richard, and Sir Perys, she was down them and in the screens passage in time to join the clot of household servants pushing out the back door into the stable yard together.

"The orchard!" someone was crying. "It was in the orchard!"

But the men from the stables who had run first to answer the scream were already coming back through the orchard gate, awkward now with whatever rake or pitchfork or stick they had caught up in their haste, and seemingly confused.

Master Payne, coming behind them, sword in one hand and Magdalen ruthlessly by the arm in the other, was not confused at all, only immensely furious.

"You've been sneaking to see *that*!" he raged. "A peddler? A damned, ragged-heeled, pass-by-the-door peddler? You couldn't find any ditch deeper to fall in, Magdalen?"

Magdalen, fighting against his hold, cried back at him, "He's my concern, not yours!"

"Not my concern—" Master Payne was choking with his anger. "My God, Magdalen, he's a *murderer*!"

"He's *not*!"

"Oliver, you're hurting her!" Mistress Payne pushed in among the press of servants. "And everyone listening! Bring her inside at least."

Master Payne had been too lost in his anger to care, but her words brought him a little back to himself. "Take her to the solar and keep her there. Jack, see to it. She's to go nowhere and not to be left alone an instant." But before he let Magdalen loose, he said into her face with set-jawed anger, "We're going to hunt your peddler down. And if we can't lay him by the heels, I can tell the sheriff what he looks like and he can do the hunting for me. The man's known around here. He won't escape."

He shoved her away toward his wife. Magdalen stumbled sideways into Mistress Payne's arms and, helpless with tears, clung to her. Frevisse reached an arm around her shoulders to help, and together she and Mistress Payne took her through the servants and into the house, Jack at their heels.

Because it seemed best to have Magdalen out of sight as soon as might be, they went up the near stairs rather than cross the hall to the others that went directly to Mistress Payne's solar. On the narrow spiral Magdalen stumbled and collapsed against Frevisse, awkwardly enough that Mistress Payne had to fall behind them, and Jack behind her. Separated from them by the turning of the stairs, Magdalen—suddenly not crying at all—whispered desperately to Frevisse, "Oliver thought he only tore his tunic, but he wounded him, I saw it. He may not be able to go far. Please find him. Help him."

"This peddler—" Frevisse began.

"He hasn't killed anyone! Trust Bess."

There was no time for more. Probably at Mistress Payne's orders, Lovie had kept the younger children inside, but they were waiting at the top of the stairs, loud with curiosity. They cut Magdalen away from Frevisse, and then Mistress Payne came, with Jack behind her and Edward and Richard crowding at his heels, Richard complaining at their father's forbidding them the hunt. They took Magdalen in an exclamatory clot toward the parlor, no one heeding that Frevisse stood quietly aside to let them go.

She went into Magdalen's room to brave Bess's and Sister Emma's frantic curiosity. Careful of every word, so as not to alarm them needlessly, she told them what apparently had happened and what had been said. There was no point in concealing any of it; Bess would have it from the other servants as soon as she joined them. But Sister Emma's exclamations of "Poor Mistress Dow" and "However do you suppose it happened?" and "Well, they certainly shouldn't leave him to roam about killing other folk, that's all I can say. A leopard can't change his spots, you know" and "A peddler! Whatever was she thinking of?" drove Frevisse close to distraction before heavy coughing and a firm insistence afterwards on a horehound drop paused Sister Emma for a while.

"You lie there quietly," Frevisse said with enforced pretense of patience, "and I'll say Sext. You can follow silently."

"Mmhmmmm," Sister Emma agreed; and fell asleep sometime before Frevisse finished.

Frevisse finished the office without faltering before rising from the bedside and saying to Bess, "Can you watch by her a while?"

"I thought I might go to Mistress Dow," Bess began.

Frevisse allowed some of her anxiety to show. "She asked me to do a task for her. She said I should trust you."

Bess opened her mouth to ask more, and then proved her worth by closing it. Instead of whatever she had been going to say in protest or ask, she simply said, "Go on then, and God go with you. She's a gentle lady, and if she asks it, it must be good."

But Magdalen's love was a peddler, though Frevisse suspected outlaw was more apt, and perhaps a murderer.

As she crossed the room she thought of bandages, and picked up the linen towel that hung beside the wash basin, rolled it small, and hid it up her habit's sleeve.

Outside the room, she moved with studied pace, careful not to seem in haste. She kept her eyes bent downward, her hands tucked into her sleeves, a familiar gesture that gave appearance of a serenity she most decidedly did not feel. If anyone asked, she was prepared to say she merely wanted a walk in the air; but she saw no one, and no one called after her as she left the house and crossed the stable yard to the orchard gate.

The orchard was silent, which gave her some hope. If Magdalen was right and her love was badly hurt, he had to have gone to earth somewhere very near. If he had, and the hunt for him had begun at the orchard edge, he was likely to have been found almost immediately. Since he had not yet been found, he had either been unhurt after all and had hared away, or else Master Payne—not knowing he was hurt— had set his hunt into the woods beyond the orchard and, moving fast to overtake him, missed him altogether.

Once into the orchard, it was not hard to guess where Magdalen had met with him; a writhe of gooseberry bushes along the stream screened a small stretch of grass from view of the house and the rest of the orchard. Frevisse wondered briefly how they had managed to meet unseen in the barren winter, and then thought that unfortunately the bushes also screened sight of anyone coming unless careful watch were kept, and that must have been how the lovers had been surprised yesterday and, most foolishly, today. Why had they risked meeting today? And how had Magdalen known he was here? For most surely she had known when she abruptly left her room. There must be some signal.

But those questions were not to her purpose. What mattered now was that Magdalen believed in her love, and both of them were more desperate than they had been before. With a sadness for how much unhappiness must have been mingled with the little joy the two of them had found in their snatched moments here, Frevisse looked around the little greensward. No broken brambles or torn grass, as there would have been from excited men searching. Nor any blood. She tried to judge where a hurt man would go to escape an armed attacker. Away from the house, surely.

Frevisse went to the clearing's lower side, where the brambles screened the stream, and found the one place through them, a narrow way probably made by deer coming for fruit in the orchard. It was wide enough for a man to slip through, a little harder for her with her skirts and veil. But she did; and found a bright smear of blood across some of the leaves at about hip level, and more on the ground further on. Magdalen had been right about him being wounded.

The way came out on the stream's bank. The stream was narrow here, its bank high on this side, low on the other. It was an easy leap for a man or a deer, and though there was a dense mix of alders and brambles on the farther bank, the narrow path through them was plain to see. With a sigh for how she would explain fresh mud on her shoes and hem, Frevisse gathered up her heavy skirts, slid down the bank, waded the stream, and slipped along the path through the bushes into the oak forest beyond them.

There was no dense undergrowth here; so close to the manor, it was undoubtedly gleaned for firewood and in the autumn grazed by the pigs. But what growth there was was unbroken and untrampled, and she judged that the hunt had not begun or come this way. Nor, to guess by the lack of blood along the deer trail, had the hurt man gone that way. Frevisse cast to either side of it, her soft shoes making faint moist sounds on the soaking ground and the wet hem of her underdress clinging to the back of her ankles as she moved. It was hard, under the day's gray overcast, to find what she needed, but finally there were broken twigs that showed where someone had passed with more haste than care, and a scuff in the mold, as if someone had slipped and regained his balance. And another brightness of blood beside the scuff. After that the signs were easier to find and follow.

They led her back toward the stream, where the bank was

still low on this side, still high on the other, running now between the forest and a meadow, with a wide band of alders on either side. Loving the water, they grew thickly here, useful for withies in building and basket-making and to hold the bank together. But they sometimes failed at the latter, and Frevisse found what looked like an excellent hiding place. At a sharp bend in the stream the bank had come down, bringing a tangle of alders with it. Still bound by roots that had not pulled completely loose, trees and turf slanted down from the upper bank to the stream, and possibly, just possibly, there was space behind them for a man to hide.

But she could not be sure of that from where she was, and after looking carefully to be sure no one was in sight, Frevisse again crossed the stream and crouched down, hidden now by the bank, near the fallen alders.

"Are you there?" she said, pitching her voice low. "Magdalen sent me. I'm here to help you."

For a moment she thought she had erred. But then something stirred in the darkness under the bank, and a low voice asked, "Dame Frevisse?"

"Evan!" she exclaimed. "How badly are you hurt? Can you come out?"

"I'll try," he said. With a slowness that betrayed pain, he drew his head and shoulders, smeared with underbank mud, into sight. "I'm hurt in my thigh. I've slowed the bleeding but I can't stop it."

"Come out if you can. Maybe I can help." She drew out the towel. "There's no one about, as nearly as I can tell. They've all gone off hunting you. Master Payne didn't realize he'd actually wounded you and they've set their search farther afield, to overtake you."

Evan managed a tight smile; but the smile narrowed into a gritted line of pain as he began to drag himself the rest of the way out. Frevisse climbed into the tangle to give what help she could, and when he was clear, made him lie on the slipped edge of the bank, near to the water, where she could both see the wound and wet the towel to clean it. Exhausted, he lay obediently still, stretched out and motionless except for shuddered, uneven breaths drawn through his clenched teeth against the pain of her tearing his ripped hosen away from the wound.

"Your hiding place has done this cut no good," Frevisse said as she began to clean the gash. "And I've nothing to cleanse it with but water." Dame Claire at St. Frideswide's used wine on the worst cuts that came to her; she claimed it kept illness out of hurts better than water did. But water was all Frevisse had for now, and she spoke to take Evan's mind at least a little away from the pain she was causing him. "But as hiding places go, and aside from the mud, it's excellent."

"Much of life is like that," Evan said in short breaths. "Excellent, except for the mud. Is Magdalen all right?"

"Except for her brother's anger, and worry over you." Frevisse inadvertently hissed as she finally saw the wound clearly. Master Payne's thrust had made a thin, deep slice across the outside of Evan's left thigh. Not so deep that the muscle was severed, but deep enough that it was still bleeding. And too high to allow the leg's amputation if the worst happened and it suppurated. If she managed to bring him to safety, it would have to be cleaned again, rigorously.

Evan lay with his face turned away, flinching now and again, his breath hissing through his clenched teeth. To cover her own sympathy Frevisse said, "Do you have any plans for your escape aside from lying here and bleeding to death?"

"If I still have the strength, I mean to go off after dark, back to camp."

"And if you don't have the strength?" Frevisse asked. She did not think he would.

"Then if it comes to my dying here, I'd likely never be found and at least they'd not have my body to hang in chains to rot at the crossroads. At least I'd spare Magdalen that."

"And leave her never knowing what became of you? If you wanted to spare her, you should have stayed away from her from the beginning."

Evan did not reply at first. Then he said, "I could have slit my throat too after I fell in love with her. It would have been the same either way. It would have killed me to deny our love once it began."

His quiet certainty, more than his words, made Frevisse pause. Almost, she could begin to believe that the love Magdalen claimed was between them was greater than its foolishness. More gently than she expected to, she said, "You can't have had hope for your love. Not with so much difference between you and her. Her family would never countenance it. And you . . ."

She did not finish; Evan knew what he was.

"I hoped not to be outlaw much longer. That would be a beginning. It's why I encouraged Nicholas to try for a pardon. Nor have I squandered everything I've 'gained.' I'd not come poor to her. And she has properties of her own. She's not dependent on her family." And then as if he read from her mind the last, greatest objection Frevisse had, their wide difference in rank, he said, "Nor was I always a peddler."

"You come of good family?"

"Good enough they wanted to see no more of me after I'd disgraced them. And seen no more of me they have. I was a stupid boy and I did stupid things, and have maybe grown only marginally wiser with the years. But yes, I come of good family. Good enough I'd be no disgrace to Magdalen." He broke off with a groan as Frevisse pressed the now-folded towel hard over the wound.

"I have to stop the bleeding," she said. "If it goes on, you will die."

Evan jerked his head in acknowledgment but did not try to speak. There was only the burble of the stream and a dripping from leaves around them as Frevisse tightened the strip of his hosen holding the towel over the wound.

When she finished, his face was gray as clay. She let him lie quietly a few moments. How much truth was in what Evan had said about himself? He clearly had better than a peasant's manners or speech about him. So maybe there was some truth to his claim of better birth.

But whether there was or not, it was not her concern. She was out here, at risk of her reputation, because Magdalen had asked her help; and having once begun to give it, Frevisse found she could not stint it.

She said, "You'll never make it so far as Nicholas's camp. And by now Master Payne probably has all the countryside roused to hunt you as Colfoot's murderer."

"I didn't kill him."

Frevisse let that go unanswered. Instead she said, "No one is likely to come this way soon. It's nearly time for supper, and their minds will be more on that than you just now. You can lie safely among the downed trees rather than crawl back into your hole and risk loosening the bandage. I'll come back for you."

Evan raised his face from his hand to look at her disbelievingly. "You can't come back! You've risked too much already. Tell Magdalen I'm all right, that the wound is nothing. Tell her—"

Frevisse gripped his shoulder. "You haven't a prayer of going far enough to be clear of the hue and cry. You move much at all with that wound and it will open again and you'll be dead by dawn and whether they hang you up at the crossroads or not, Magdalen's heart will grieve her to her grave."

Wincing a little under the force of both her grip and her words, Evan nodded.

Unrelenting, Frevisse went on. "Then listen to me. I don't think you killed Colfoot. But Master Payne very desperately wants us to believe you did. We must keep you alive and clear you or no one will ever look for the true murderer. We can't keep you alive out here." Not with more rain coming. Not without shelter and warmth and food.

"If Nicholas knew, he'd come for me."

"I've no way to send him word. Do you?"

"No."

"Then that's no help. For now, let me help you back among the trees."

Evan took the pain and effort of moving in grim silence. But when he was lying among the trees on the slanted fall of bank, hidden well enough for now, he said, "This is odd repayment for the trouble I brought you into with Nicholas."

Frevisse had not thought of it as payment or repayment. She hesitated, surprised, then answered, "You said you were a stupid boy. Let's just suppose that I'm a stupid woman and so here I am. Stay alive until I come for you."

Chapter
16

THE HEAVY OVERCAST would bring early dark, hopefully at supper time when all the household would be gathered in the hall and kitchen. That would be her best chance for bringing Evan into the house. She already knew where she would hide him, but in the meanwhile there was the rest of the afternoon to pass, her own muddy dress to be explained, and Sister Emma to be considered.

Her dress was no problem. "I slipped in a muddy place and fell," she said, first to the servant Lovie, meeting her as she came in the door, and then to Sister Emma, awake and upright in the bed. Bess wanted to have the dress off her, to clean again; Frevisse, aware that she was only going to dirty it again, insisted a simple brushing would be enough for now. Bess did not press her, but Sister Emma, interrupted only by her frequent coughing, chattered on about how inconvenient it was to become ill while traveling and wasn't it a wonder none of her family had come yet to visit her and . . .

But it was for another reason Frevisse asked Bess if there were any more of Mistress Payne's poppy syrup to hand.

To deliberately drug Sister Emma insensible was a desperate measure. Frevisse tried to convince herself that if

161

everything were carefully explained to her, Sister Emma would hold her tongue. But when Bess brought the drink of poppy syrup mixed in warm, spiced wine, Frevisse took it and set it by the bed. "Here's your medicine, sister. No, wait. Shall we say Vespers first?"

"Oh, no. Let me take it now. Never put off till tomorrow what can be done today. This cough wakes me, you know, every time I'm almost asleep. No, I'll have the medicine. The drink will stop my coughing for Vespers, and when we've finished I can sleep."

Frevisse gave her the drink. Sister Emma drank deeply and with enjoyment. Then they crossed themselves and began Vespers' opening antiphon. " '*Deus, in adjutorium meum intende.*' " O God, come to my aid; make haste, O Lord, to help me.

The office was brief, but Sister Emma was asleep well before the final psalm. Frevisse, rising from her knees, turned to find Bess waiting behind her and said, "Find out where everyone is and how long they're likely to be there."

Bess looked at with barely held curiosity, but only said, "Yes, my lady," and left.

When she was gone, Frevisse carefully smoothed the blankets over Sister Emma and drew the bed curtains. Then there was nothing left to do but pace the room with her own thoughts, go to the window to watch the gray evening thicken toward darkness, and listen for Bess's return.

By the time she came, Frevisse had begun to sicken with worry. She tucked her hands up her sleeves to hide their trembling as Bess entered, a little breathless with haste, carrying three suppers on a tray. "I had to wait to bring this," she explained. "I said you wanted to stay with Sister Emma and had asked me to keep company with you, but I couldn't think why I shouldn't wait to bring this back. That's what took so long. Everyone's going into supper now, except Adam is keeping watch on Magdalen in the solar."

Then everyone was safe enough out of the way for a while. Frevisse prayed to God it would be for long enough.

"Bess, there's something we have to do."

It had the elements of a nightmare. The silent escape from the house into the glooming twilight. Finding the way back through the orchard and along the stream. And the fear that Evan would not be there.

But he was, though chilled, damp, so stiffened he could hardly rise even with their help, and barely able to hobble when they had him on his feet. The return to the house seemed to go on forever, with the danger that supper would end before they reached there. Or that Evan's strength would give out and they would be unable to carry him.

They reached the back door at last, unseen so far as they knew and with Evan still on his feet. Leaving him sagged against the wall, Frevisse cautiously opened the door to the screens passage, listening for every sound until she could see there was no one there. Subdued talk from the hall told her supper continued; but anyone might pass at any time—from the kitchen with another course, or from the hall with empty dishes. Tense with fear and the desire for haste where there could be no haste, she and Bess brought Evan into the passage and to the shadows at the foot of the stairway.

His strength was nearly gone by then. He fell forward onto his hands and knees on the steps, Frevisse grabbing him under the arm only at the last instant to break his fall and stop him from landing noisily.

"You have to go up," she whispered, pulling on him. "We can't carry you. You must go up."

He did, with agonizing slowness, Frevisse beside him—she seemed to be perpetually helping someone up these stairs—Bess behind, pushing as best she could. Near the top they paused to listen, but there was no sound.

"The door," Frevisse gasped. Evan was leaning nearly his

full weight against her now; she could do nothing more than hold him. Bess squeezed past them to open Magdalen's door, shivering with her own nervousness, then came to Evan's other side to help bring him in. Hardly believing they had done it, Frevisse ordered, "Close it," but Bess already was doing so, gasping out a thankful prayer that echoed Frevisse's silent one as that slight barrier closed between them and immediate danger.

"The truckle bed," Frevisse said. "The one along the wall."

Because the great bed stood so high, the truckle bed on its far side was hidden from the door. Unless someone walked well into the room, anyone lying there would be unseen. And if there was no way to prevent someone coming in, the truckle bed with Evan on it could be shoved under again. So long as he was quiet, he would have some degree of safety, at least for a little while.

Together, she and Bess lowered him onto the bed, ignoring what his filthy, bloody clothing would do to the sheets. Evan lay back, unable to hold in a heavy groan as finally he let his body go limp. Bess went to light a lamp. When she brought it back to hold over the bed, Frevisse finally saw him clearly and was appalled by his pallor, the gray around his shut eyes. He had lost far too much blood. He needed food, but more than that, he needed liquids. And the strength to drink them. A strength she was not sure he had.

Praying silently for God's help and mercy, she managed to get wine in him first, holding the cup to his lips and encouraging him to drink. She hoped that wine did a wound as much good from the inside as it did from the outside. At least it brought a trace of color back to his face, and she said to Bess, "Bring me the ale from the supper tray, and Sister Emma's broth."

With her help Evan drank the ale, but when she tried to

spoon some of the broth into him, he turned his head away with a groan.

"Hush!" Frevisse whispered fervently. "You'll be heard!" She regretted that she had given all the poppy syrup to Sister Emma. And she did not know what they could do for bandages; blood was soaking through her makeshift one. But that could wait a little while; she had to keep Evan from slipping into death from sheer weakness.

"Eat," she hissed at him. "Magdalen doesn't want to find you dead beside her bed. Eat this."

She forced the spoon against his teeth and he roused enough to make the effort. A little of the broth went down him, and a little more.

When there was more color in his face—still not much but better than the deathly gray he had had at first—she turned to his wound. Rather than disturb it by taking off the soaked towel, she folded another and placed it on top of the first. She was only half finished tying it in place when the door latch rattled. Panic and her heart leaped into Frevisse's throat. She and Bess sprang to their feet, looking frantically for something they could do to seem natural and yet keep themselves between the bed and the door.

But Jack barely glanced at them as he came in and held the door wide for Magdalen to enter.

"I'll be outside all night," he said to her, a little shame-faced but definite. "You know you're not to leave. I'd have to stop you and tell Master Payne if you try."

With her quiet dignity, Magdalen said, "I know. He made it very plain. I won't give you any trouble."

"That's all right then," Jack said. He ducked his head at Frevisse. "You can come and go as you choose, of course, my lady."

"Thank you," Frevisse said, forcing a smile, her voice only a little strained.

"Well, then," said Jack. He found he had nothing else to

say under the unwavering regard of three women, and retreated, shutting the door behind him.

"Oh, my lady!" Bess burst out, hurrying toward Magdalen, who held up a hand to ward her off.

"If you're kind, I'll begin to cry, and once I do, I won't be able to stop," she said. Then her gaze fell toward Bess's feet. Her eyes widened and she looked sharply toward Frevisse's. "You're both all muddy. How did you come to be all muddy?"

"Magdalen—" Frevisse began warningly.

But Magdalen had been running the narrow ridge between hope and despair for too many hours. Her control was finally breaking. Keeping her voice low, she demanded in pain, "Did you find him? Is he alive? Where is he?"

Frevisse moved to intercept her, ready to cover her mouth if she cried out any louder. "He's here. He's hurt just as you thought but he's—"

Magdalen was now far enough into the room to see past Frevisse to the truckle bed. With a great indrawn breath, she rushed to fall on her knees beside him in the narrow space between bed and wall. He lifted a hand to her weakly. She grasped it in both her own and bent over him, speaking too low for anyone but him to hear but looking between laughter and tears with gladness and fear.

Evan raised his other hand to stroke his fingers gently from her forehead down her cheek. "It's only slight," he said softly. "It will mend." Magdalen buried her face between his neck and shoulder; he slid his arm around her shoulders, holding her as best he could.

Frevisse let them have their moment, then said, "The wound needs to be cleansed. He needs to be rid of those filthy clothes and warmed and fed. Can you help us do that?"

"Yes," Magdalen said fervently. "Yes." She straightened, wiping tears from her eyes. "There's food here. Good. And there's a shirt of Edward's I was mending that he can wear. And we can use the linen I have for a new underdress for bandages. Bess, warm me as much more water as we have and there's ointment among my medicines in that chest over there." With Evan in her care and her worst fear lessened, she was her confident self again. "Dame Frevisse, I know this isn't work for you. Will you pray for us while I do it?"

Frevisse forbore to say that the bandage on Evan's thigh was her doing and that she had helped Dame Claire tend to hurt men from the village more than once. She simply nodded and went to sit on a stool near the door. Better that even for this little while Magdalen be too busy to think about how much in danger they all were, and most especially Evan.

Chapter

17

BESS WAS AS deeply asleep as Sister Emma, and all sounds through the house except the rain against the window had stopped. Frevisse had no way to know the hour, except that it was late, or very early, but sleep had not come yet to her or Magdalen; and now that Evan had roused from one of his brief rests, the three of them were talking close together over things that had to be said.

They had put out all lights in the room but a single low-burning lamp near the foot of the bed where Bess slept. With food and Magdalen's care, Evan had recovered strength enough to lie propped up against his pillows. He was clean now, and cleanly clad in Edward's shirt; the lamplight gave a golden color to his face, and almost he might have looked well. But he lay with the sunken stillness of the very ill, and Magdalen sitting beside him never let loose his hand, as if afraid she would lose him if she did.

And very well she might, whether she held on to him or not.

Frevisse thought that if the wound did not infect he would heal well enough. He required only time. But he would never have that time if he were discovered.

"If there were some way to convince Oliver that Evan is

innocent," Magdalen said. "Or if we could smuggle him out of the house, now that his wound is tended."

Frevisse doubted Magdalen believed any more than she did in the chance of persuading her brother to spare Evan once he laid hands on him. Oliver Payne's fury had been too deep, his determination too certain. As for spiriting Evan away, only driven necessity and good luck had enabled them to bring him here. They could not depend on those again. And even if they could, any movement would risk re-opening the wound, and Evan could not lose much more blood and live.

"If there were some way Nicholas could know what had happened, he might come for me," Evan said.

"And convince Master Payne to free you?" Frevisse asked quellingly. "Does he even know you're one of Nicholas's men?"

Magdalen made a small, quickly checked movement as Evan answered, "No. It seemed better that Nicholas be the only one of us Payne knew. That way I could keep some watch on what was toward with Payne's own concerns without him knowing I mattered."

Softly, urgently, Magdalen said, "Dame Frevisse, you *know* what Evan is?"

Startled, Frevisse realized she had assumed Magdalen was innocent of what Evan was; and apparently Magdalen had assumed the same of her. "*You* know?" she echoed.

Magdalen laughed quietly. "That he's an outlaw? Yes. That his family cast him off for a foolishness he readily admits, and that he was a peddler and then fell in with outlaws and is their spy? Yes. He told me all that when we first began to be in love."

Pain from deeper than his outward wound showed in Evan's face. "I came here with no intent but to find the best way to coerce her brother to our use. I never expected her.

And when I'd found her, I didn't want a lie between us. Even if it meant I lost her afterward."

Magdalen's smile had all the pleasure of heart-held memories. "We met by chance in the yard one day, when he was persuading Lovie that Mistress Payne would find his sewing needles the finest to be had. I had lost all but my last needle and we fell to talking. The talk went past needles to other things, and I found him to be more than he appeared. And when he came again, I made reason to talk with him more. When next he came, we went into the orchard, to be out of the way of the come and go of the yard. He came more often after that, and we arranged how he would let me know when he was near, or we would set a day and time. I had often walked in the orchard alone before then. I don't think anyone even suspected I had more reason to walk there then."

Drawn into her memories, Evan said, smiling with her, "Though winter made it difficult. No leaves on the trees to hide us."

"So we could only talk while he was in the house, trying to sell his wares, with others all around us. In the kitchen, usually."

"At least I was well fed those days."

They laughed softly, their heads close together. They had had very little, but given all their hearts to it.

"But that's no help now," Frevisse said.

The brief gladness went out of them. Magdalen straightened, still holding his hand. "How do you know about him? And about this Nicholas and his dealings with my brother?"

"Nicholas is my cousin, though I've not seen him in sixteen years. Evan helped him seize me a few days ago so they could persuade me to write my uncle about a pardon for Nicholas and all his men."

"Pardon?" Magdalen looked from her to Evan and back again with quickened hope. "He could be pardoned?"

"My uncle has the power to obtain pardons, yes. I wrote him about it the morning after I arrived here. Your brother knows about this."

"But if Evan is to be pardoned—"

"For his outlawry," Frevisse interrupted. "I never wrote anything about murder."

"He didn't murder Colfoot!"

"I don't think your brother means for him to live long enough to prove that one way or the other. If he's found here, he's dead and pardon won't even be a question to be raised."

The night's silence closed around her words. Magdalen closed her eyes and looked ill, but she did not deny it. Evan turned his head away. Frevisse gazed toward a shadowed corner with no idea at all what they should do next. The silence drew on until, not looking up, Magdalen said, "We must find a way to force Oliver to let Evan go."

Frevisse and Evan both looked toward her. "Evan, you've told me Oliver invests the money that Nicholas brings him. The money you 'gather' from other people."

"My share of it and Nicholas's," Evan agreed. "Though Oliver thinks it's only Nicholas's."

"And he keeps record of it," said Magdalen. "Oliver keeps record of everything."

"Nicholas says he's seen a roll with our profits on it, yes," Evan agreed.

But Frevisse protested, "Your brother wouldn't keep a record of his dealings with outlaws, would he?"

"This Nicholas is known around here as a forester," Magdalen answered. "People suspect otherwise, but no one's challenged the tale. So long as Oliver claims he thought he was dealing with an honest man over honest money, he can't be in trouble for it." She stopped, opened her mouth to speak, stopped again, then finally said in a strained voice, "Oliver is not always honest. And if he were ever going to cheat someone, it would be Nicholas, an outlaw likely to be killed or caught before he could call Oliver to account. Someone unable to make claim against him."

Evan stared at her. "He wouldn't dare cheat Nicholas!"

"If ever he cheated anyone, it would be Nicholas," Magdalen countered. "Oliver detests him. He thinks Nicholas is a fool. I think he thinks worse things about him too, but has never said them."

"But when Nicholas has his pardon and comes for his money, what will Payne say?" Evan asked. "That he's sorry but there isn't any?"

"That there have been losses. That there's not as much as Nicholas had hoped for."

"And what will Nicholas do even if he disbelieves him?" Frevisse put in. "Harm Payne and forfeit his pardon? Take him to court to sue for money had through extortions and robbery? If only we had something we could use, something that might put Master Payne in Nicholas's mercy . . ." Frevisse abruptly realized what she had been saying—and thinking—about Nicholas. He was a liar, she knew, a thief, an extortionist, and some part of her doubted deeply he had had any change of heart. Did she truly want to put Master Payne in his power?

"But we don't have anything," Evan said flatly.

"Yes, we do," Magdalen answered quietly. Her face was bleak with the knowledge that she was betraying her brother. "I didn't know you had hope of a pardon, but you'd told me about the money that Oliver was supposed to be investing it for you. I knew you hoped to use it for us to have a life together, so that you'd not be dependent on what I have—though there's sufficient."

Evan began to answer her but she cupped her hand against his cheek, stopping his protest. "I know," she said softly. "You wanted more for us. You've said it before. So

I worried and I . . ." She drew a deep, trembling breath. ". . . stole the key that Oliver leaves with Iseult when he's gone beyond a day. I opened the chest and took the roll that has to do with Nicholas."

"What's in it?" Frevisse asked. "You still have it?"

For answer, Magdalen rose and went to one of her own chests along the wall. She reached deeply under the clothing folded there and brought out a tightly rolled scroll.

As Madgalen handed her the scroll, Frevisse asked, "Are you sure about the cheating?"

Magdalen picked up the lamp to cast its light down on them for better reading. "There are two sheets together. Look at them both."

At first perusal, the accounts were straightforward enough. A listing of dates alongside sums received from Nicholas and sums invested in various ventures, with an occasional comment on a specific return from a particular effort. In fact there was a steady increment of money all through the first sheet. But on the second sheet there began to be steep losses, and the comments next to them were terser. Frevisse did not take time for a careful assessment, but gathered the impression that as of the first of this month Nicholas's money was reduced to hardly more than what he had put into Master Payne's hands over the period of several years; almost all his profits had vanished in less than five months.

"Oh," she said.

"Oh indeed," Evan agreed dryly. She had held the scrolls up for the light. Now she realized he had been reading them with her, and her face must have betrayed her surprise, for he said, "I told you I came of good family. As a younger son, I was trained to be of use around my father's manor. Stuck in a room to keep the records, as it happened, and it didn't suit me, but I learned to read. Nicholas will not like those figures."

"What Nicholas truly won't like is this." Frevisse ran her finger down the length of the second sheet. "Is this what you meant?" she asked Magdalen.

Magdalen nodded. "The ink is all the same. All the entries from January on were written at once."

Evan sucked in his breath sharply through his teeth. "Ah! I'd missed that! Let me see."

He took the first sheet. On it the darkness of the ink was different from one entry to the next because Master Payne had written one entry at a time, dried it, and not written another until some other day, with another pen and often a noticeably different ink since it was difficult to make one batch of ink identical to another. But the second page was uniform in ink and pen from the first entry to nearly the last. Only the final two entries were varied. Except for those, the page had been done all at once. And that page recorded all the losses.

Frevisse looked at the paper assessingly. Payne was a cheat; could he perhaps also be a murderer? Was that why he was so determined to cast Evan as the criminal? Slowly, she told herself. She must go through these facts slowly.

"When did Nicholas begin to speak of a pardon?" Frevisse asked.

"I began trying to move him to it last autumn," Evan said. "But it took the harsh winter to decide him. He first spoke of it as his own idea around February, I'd guess."

"And about then he probably told Master Payne," Frevisse said, "who didn't like the thought of losing all the money he had been earning for someone he despised. So he changed the roll. And I doubt Nicholas would have noticed. He's ever more interested in final amounts than details. He would have raged but accepted it. What happens if we send these to him with a letter explaining you need rescuing and here's the threat he needs to hold over Master Payne's head to do it?"

"He'll come," Evan said certainly. "He likes the notion of himself as a gallant leader, ready to dare all for his men—so long as we don't too greatly inconvenience him, for then his interest wanes. Taking me out of here will be inconvenient, but since he will come to rage at Payne, rescuing me will be hardly more effort. He'll come and he'll enjoy bullying Payne, and carrying me off from under his nose will be an added insult. But we have to put this into his hands first."

"I can take a horse from the stable," Magdalen said, "and go wherever you tell me."

"You will not!" said Evan, startled.

"You're watched," said Frevisse. "It would raise too much alarm and risk Evan being found."

"Then you go," Magdalen urged Frevisse.

But as Frevisse hesitated at the danger and impropriety. Evan said, "It doesn't have to go to the camp. Odds are one of our men will be at the Wheatsheaf, the alehouse in the village, sometime tomorrow—today. In this weather, they tire of the woods and want some pleasure. Old Nan is to be trusted. She's the alewife. If she's given something to hand on to Nicholas, she'll do it. If you could take this to her, Dame Frevisse—"

But Frevisse liked the idea of traveling alone to an alehouse only a little better than going in search of the outlaw camp alone.

"Bess can do it!" Magdalen exclaimed. "No one will question her going."

She had set the lamp down, and now reached out to clasp Evan's pale hand lying on the blankets. A warmth of hope shone in her eyes strongly enough that it seemed to kindle a little in him. Here was a somewhat better chance, dependent on keeping Evan hidden only until Nicholas came for him.

The lamp flickered in the last of its oil. The rain was loud again in their silence. And after a moment Frevisse said,

"We should sleep if we may. Magdalen, will you come into the bed beside Sister Emma?"

Magdalen tightened her hand around Evan's. "No. I'll sleep here."

With forced lightness, Evan said, "I've no sword to put between us, to assure your virtue."

"I think your wound does that sufficiently," Magdalen answered, matching his lightness. And then with no lightness at all but her whole heart in her eyes, she said, "Evan, I want to be nowhere tonight except as near you as I may. This one night. Please."

Evan's answer was in his eyes as clearly as her longing was in hers; he shifted as best he awkwardly could to the farther side of the narrow bed, and held up the blankets for her. With a simplicity beyond modesty, Magdalen slipped in beside him. Careful of his hurt, she nestled against him, her head on his shoulder, her arm across his chest. Eyes closing, he let his cheek sink against her dark hair, and they settled into what rest there could be for them that night.

Quietly Frevisse put out the light and rose to make her way into bed beside Sister Emma.

There had been a time, when she was very young, when she had thought to love and be loved much as they loved now. But realities and a greater love had come between her and then. She was long past regretting it; could not even remember if she had regretted it for very long—her decision now seemed so inevitable.

But seeing Magdalen with Evan in the small happiness they had made for themselves, she wished there could be more for them than the little they had had; more than the little that was likely to be all they would ever have.

The room's darkness wrapped around her as she felt her way silently between the sheets. There was nothing more that could be done until the morning. She could only let everything go until then. Everything except her prayers.

Almost without thinking about it, she drifted into the prayers of Matins and Lauds, chanting them silently in her mind. Her need was suddenly overwhelming. She wanted to be in St. Frideswide's church, secure among the other nuns, her voice rising with theirs among the familiar shadows and the smells of incense, oil, candles, and herb-strewed rushes.

Improperium exspectavit cor meum et miseriam . . . consolantem me quaesivi, et non inveni. I feared my heart would break with shame and sorrow . . . I begged someone to comfort me, and found no one.

Where had that psalm come from? Not part of Matins or Lauds, but very much to the point after all. She finished with the Paternoster; and its ending, *sed libera nos a malo,* caught and repeated itself in her mind, over and over. But deliver us from evil, from evil, from evil. Amen, amen.

Chapter

❧18❧

Frevisse was drawn from unsatisfying sleep by Sister Emma's stir and snuffle into wakefulness beside her. Trying to avoid both Sister Emma and her own thoughts, she buried herself deeper into the bed and blankets. But it was no use. Sister Emma groaned and flung her hand out, slapping into Frevisse's back.

"Willo birdie sush," she murmured. "Uh, oh, fursh!"

Frevisse sat up and turned to her. "Sister Emma, wake up. You're dreaming." She laid a hand on her shoulder; the sheet and blanket were wet. Quickly she felt Sister Emma's forehead and called out, "Bess, come! Her fever has broken!"

Sister Emma stretched, coming more awake, shoving the blankets away from her. Frevisse pulled them back up to her neck. "No, you must stay covered, you're all damp," she urged. Among the things they did not need right now was for Sister Emma to take another chill.

Bess, already dressed and neat for the day that was no more yet than a gray glooming between the shutters, drew open the curtains on Sister Emma's side of the bed. She felt sister Emma's forehead as Frevisse had and said, "It's broken indeed. She'll be much better now, poor lady."

179

"Ohhhh," Sister Emma said, more fully awaked. "I'm so *wet*. What's happened?"

"Your fever has broken, my lady," Bess repeated. "You'll be better now."

Out of sight below Frevisse's side of the bed, Magdalen stirred. There was rustling and then the rumble of the truckle bed being rolled under the higher bed. Frevisse hoped Evan could bear cramped spaces.

"I don't feel better," Sister Emma complained. Her breathing was short, her voice clogged.

"You want something to drink," Bess assured her. "You're sweating like—" She thought better of whatever comparison had come to her. "Your body is exhausting itself. You must lie quietly and drink as much as you can. Here."

She deftly pulled up the covers Sister Emma was trying to push away, and held a cup to her mouth, distracting her.

"What is it?" Sister Emma demanded. "I don't want any more medicine. I've had such dreams. . . ."

"It's just ale, my lady. Not even spices in it. See? Taste it."

Bess seemed to have the matter well in hand. Relieved, Frevisse sat up as Magdalen straightened from beside the bed. Their eyes met briefly, acknowledging what they faced today, before Sister Emma burbled, "Yes, that does feel better. You're right. I need more to drink. I'm perishing of thirst."

Her face was shining pink with perspiration, and her short hair stood up in damp golden ringlets. But she was definitely in better health than yesterday. As she lowered the cup from another deep drink, she said, "Good morning, Mistress Dow! I'm so much better today, it's quite exceptional! I seem to have slept forever. They say that a night's good sleep is worth a week of rest. Oh, I do want out of this bed for a while."

"No!" Frevisse and Magdalen chorused.

"No," Frevisse repeated. "For nothing except necessity. You still have congestion."

"But it's much improved," Sister Emma protested, and coughed to demonstrate how much.

"We want it to improve even more," Frevisse persisted. "I really think you'll have to have more medicine." She did not see how they would survive the day with Sister Emma conscious and talking the entire time. Aside from all else, they needed her asleep again so that Evan could be fed, his wound seen to, and nature answered.

She turned to Magdalen. "Do you suppose Mistress Payne would allow us just a little more of her syrup?"

"I really don't want—" Sister Emma began.

"Here's more ale, my lady," Bess interrupted. As she held the cup for Sister Emma to drink again, she looked across the bed at Frevisse and shook her head.

Frevisse understood she should let the matter rest. "I had best dress," she said, and rose to do so. Her gown had been cleaned as well it could be by Bess last night, and she had slept in her chemise as St. Benedict's Holy Rule required. Now she dressed and pinned her veil into place while Bess—leaving Sister Emma with the cup refilled with ale—helped Magdalen dress and put up her hair and veil it.

In every outward way it was simply a usual morning; and that was how they had to make it appear to Sister Emma. Sipping her ale, she chattered and occasionally coughed, and sank lower on the pillows moment by moment. Watching her closely, Bess plucked the cup from her hands just before she subsided completely into sleep. Between one moment and the next she was oblivious, her mouth a little open, her eyes heavily shut, her head sagged sideways on the pillow.

"How did you manage?" Magdalen whispered at Bess.

"Good drink often takes a body that way after a fever has

broken," Bess whispered back, plainly pleased with herself.

"Did you have any of the poppy syrup in the ale?" Frevisse asked.

Bess looked guilty. "I didn't dare. There's only a little left from yesterday and I stole that."

"Bess!" Magdalen exclaimed.

"I didn't dare ask Mistress Payne for more! She said when she gave me some the first day that there should be only one dose at a time and days and days before there was another one. If she knew we wanted more, she'd want to come see Sister Emma for herself, and then maybe refuse the syrup after all."

Magdalen patted her arm. "Then you did right. We'll save what little syrup there is in case of dire need."

There was a rap at the door, and without opening it Adam called, "The family's gathering for prayers and breakfast! Mistress is asking if Dame Frevisse is coming?"

Frevisse drew in her breath impatiently. "The letter to Nicholas isn't written yet," she said in a low voice to Magdalen.

"I'll do it. I know what to say. Best you go down, tell them that everything is well here, learn what you can."

Frevisse raised her voice to reach Adam. "I'll be there at once!"

She paused a moment to gather herself. She had never faced so many people with so great a deception. Bess, looking as subdued as Frevisse felt, followed her from the room, down the stairs, and went to the kitchen to fetch back breakfasts that would mostly go to Evan, while Frevisse went on to the hall.

Fearing she was delaying the Paynes' morning prayers, she went rapidly to stand at her place at the head table, beside Mistress Payne. Despite Bess's report of Sir Perys's lengthy prayers yesterday, today he went at a brisk pace, finishing them before anyone but Bartholomew and Kate became restless. When he had finished, everyone sat.

There was no need for serving; the ale and yesterday's bread and cold meats from supper were already set out on the tables. Breakfast was a meal with scant ceremony and little time given to it because dinner, the main meal of the day, was only four or five hours away, and the morning's work was waiting. So talk was slight and no one dawdled over their food, but Frevisse learned that there was no word yet as to when the sheriff and crowner would arrive, and that Master Payne had indeed called out the hue and cry on Evan yesterday. By now word would be spread far and wide to be on the watch for a peddler well known through the neighborhood.

Frevisse also judged that Master Payne was in a seething temper. He contained it well; his movements were as precise and set as they had ever been, but his face was drawn with an in-held tension that was costing him much effort. And Mistress Payne's anxious sideways looks at him showed how acutely she felt his strain.

Because breakfast was so casual, Edward and Richard sat at table on their father's left. Edward appeared caught in the side-lash of his father's ill temper; there were both worry and wariness in the looks he dodged toward him. Richard seemed equally subdued, concentrating on his food, and at the lower tables so were Katherine and Richard and the servants, though they were perhaps not so tense. Only Kate and Bartholomew seemed unconcerned. And Frevisse suspected Sir Perys's brooding silence was probably centered more on the coming tribulation of morning lessons than anything else.

At the end of the meal, Frevisse thanked Mistress Payne, and assured her that Sister Emma was much improved but was best left to rest, and that Magdalen had had a quiet night and was no more distressed than was reasonable, and that she would certainly ask for anything Sister Emma might need.

She finally made her escape with great relief, only to have to face Adam sitting on a stool outside Magdalen's door. With a pretense of normal manners she asked, "Have you eaten? Should I bring you something?"

"Nay. I ate before I came up, but thanks for the kindness. How is it with her?" He nodded toward Magdalen's door. "Bess wouldn't say aught except she's well and it's none of our business, she's not our lady. But we like her. All the household does."

Surprised she could say it so easily, Frevisse answered, "She does well enough. It will be better when this is past."

"That it will," Adam agreed. "Master Payne has sent two messages to the sheriff in haste, and means to have the countryside roused for miles round today in hunt for this fellow. It'll be best for all when it's settled and he's dead."

"Indeed," Frevisse agreed, sick in her heart. "The door, please?"

He let her in and shut it behind her.

From the bed Sister Emma said, "There you are. Do you know, we haven't said Prime yet. Or at least *I* haven't. Have you? I'm feeling much the better for my little nap. Do you want to say the office now?"

Her mind elsewhere, Frevisse groped and said awkwardly, "In a moment. I need to talk to Mistress Dow."

Magdalen was sitting at the window where the poor daylight was best, pretending to sew. Frevisse crossed to her, glancing quickly around the room to see that Bess was gone, and leaned casually over Magdalen's shoulder as if interested in the embroidery. "Mistress Payne sends you her well-wishes."

"What news? Is everyone well?"

"Everyone is fine," Frevisse assured her. "And nothing has changed since yesterday, except there's word come that

Colfoot's people should be here maybe late this afternoon to take his body away as soon as the sheriff and crowner are done with it."

"Are they here yet? The sheriff and the crowner?"

"No. We don't know when they're expected." She leaned closer to inspect her work in more detail. "What very fine stitches you do. And the colors are so clear. Is it your own dye?" Too low for Sister Emma to hear, she added, "Bess is gone with the letter?"

"It's something of Iseult's. She's very clever with dyes and that sort of thing." In a whisper she added, "Yes."

"I met her when I first came, didn't I," Sister Emma said from the bed. "Mistress Payne. A little woman, I remember. Very kind. I do want to see her again and thank her for all her kindness. Gratitude is the poor man's payment, and ingratitude is . . ." She paused to cough, and finished more feebly. "I forget what"—she coughed again—"but something anyway."

Frevisse looked across to her with alarm, then asked Magdalen, "Has she taken the medicine yet?"

Magdalen shook her head. "I offered it a few minutes ago and she refused it. She says she wants her wits about her for a while, she's weary of sleeping." Her voice dropped. "And I haven't been able to see to Evan."

"Merciful God," Frevisse breathed. They could not have Sister Emma awake for much longer. With seeming casualness she went to her and said, "Do you want to do Prime now?"

"I think so. I've missed so many of the offices these past few days, it's a scandal."

"I doubt Father Henry will demand penance for it. You've been ill."

"I'm still ill," Sister Emma said with a trace of peevishness. She fretted at the covers. "I don't feel well at all."

"Would you like your medicine?"

"No. I told you, I'm tired of sleeping."

She was definitely improving, if return to her usual single-mindedness was any sign.

"Well, you probably know best," Frevisse said, but with a cast of doubt. She studied Sister Emma's face intently. "You're very pale now that your fever is gone. Are you sure you're better?"

"I feel much better. Only a little achy. But that could be from so much time abed, don't you think?"

"Very likely," Frevisse agreed, still allowing doubt to show in her voice. "Shall we do Prime now?"

"I do think that will help me," Sister Emma said.

They bowed their heads for the opening hymn, which was less impressive when recited in a swift undertone than when sung by many voices in the choir: " '*Jam lucis orto sidere, Deum precemur supplices, Ut in diurnis actibus Nos servet a nocentibus.*' " Now in the sun's new dawning ray, Lowly of heart, our God we pray That He from harm may keep us free In all the deeds this day shall see.

Frevisse, all too aware of how much responsibility she bore for what was happening and might happen today, prayed that with edged awareness.

At the end of the office, Emma was still looking very alert. But Frevisse, desperate, leaned over her as if concerned, and said, "You're so pale, as if all your strength has wasted out of you. I'm sure you need more rest than you think you do. Are you sure you don't want your medicine? To help you rest?"

"Really, I—" Sister Emma began indignantly, but a coughing fit cut off her words and left her lying weakly against her pillows, breathless.

And given that opportunity, Frevisse simply picked up the cup sitting on the bedside table, lifted Emma with one arm, and held the cup to her lips.

Helpless from the coughing, Sister Emma drank. When

she had finished, Frevisse settled her back against the pillows and patted her shoulder. "You'll feel better than you believe when you wake."

Sister Emma sighed. "I do hope so. I really feel so foolish, being this ill. It was all that rain in the woods. I hated that. Drip, drip, drip, drip, all wet and cold."

Her voice drifted on. They waited, and in a while she faded into silence, her eyelids flickering. They waited longer, and her breathing and face evened into sleep.

"What else could we do?" Magdalen asked. But she was not interested in an answer, and was already moving to roll the truckle bed out into the light again.

Evan was awake, gray with weariness and pain, but he reached to clasp her hand in wordless reassurance that he was still there.

His wound had not worsened in the night. When Magdalen eased off the bandages, it was a clean line, ugly with raw edges but not discolored. She washed it with wine, as she had before, and re-covered it. "You have to lie as still as may be, to keep from opening it," she said, and kissed his forehead.

His crooked face eased toward a smile. "Lying still is no trouble at all," he assured her.

She fed him then, as much as she could persuade him to eat, from her breakfast and Bess's. When that was done and there was nothing left but the waiting, Evan took her hand and drew her down to sit on the floor beside the bed. They did not speak, but stayed there hand in hand. Frevisse, who had kept close to give Magdalen anything she might need, went to sit near the door, on the chance of anyone entering, and tried to pray, but remained more aware of Magdalen and Evan and of every sound beyond the door.

But nonetheless she started to her feet when a knock came, even took a step forward, then swung around to be sure Magdalen was having no trouble sliding the truckle bed away. Her hand on the latch to slow anyone trying to enter, she waited until Magdalen stood away from the bed, then composed her face and opened the door.

Adam was standing to one side, irresolutely muttering, "Master said no one's to go in." Mistress Payne, directly in the doorway, was ignoring him, though there was uncertainty in every line of her face and body as she wrung her hands, fighting the gesture even as she did it, and said to Frevisse, "Oliver has said we're to leave Magdalen alone until this is all finished, but I have to see Sister Emma, see how she is."

She sounded as if she expected to be sent away on the instant, but from across the room Magdalen said warmly, "Iseult, come in," and held out her arms.

Relieved to be welcomed, and with a quelling glance at Adam, Mistress Payne came to her. They embraced and then, still holding Magdalen, she leaned back to look up into her face as Frevisse went to stand quietly out of the way, between Iseult and the bed.

"I've begged Oliver to show you mercy but there's nothing he wants to hear," Mistress Payne said. "He's furious. You've been meeting this man for a long while, haven't you?"

"You knew?" Magdalen asked.

"I—thought there was—someone." Her sister-in-law moved away from her nervously. "I—hoped there was someone. But I never thought. . . . Oh, Magdalen, a peddler? You couldn't find anyone else to love but a peddler? Are you that unhappy here?"

Magdalen went after her to put her arms around her again. "I've never been unhappy here! That wasn't it. I wasn't looking to be in love. But it happened and there's nothing about him that I'm ashamed of. Nor anything we've done that I would hide from Oliver, except I know he's someone Oliver will never accept."

Gravely Mistress Payne said, "How can any of us accept him, Magdalen? He's a murderer."

Magdalen lifted her head defiantly. "That isn't proven, he's only accused; and it isn't true."

"Then why won't he come out of hiding? Surely he must know he's wanted. The hue and cry has gone all around."

"What he knows is that Oliver is in a rage against him. No, better he stay free, whatever comes of it. And even if I never see him again, that's enough for me. To know he's safe."

Mistress Payne cried out in distress at so much defiance, "Oh, Magdalen!" as if she were about to weep.

Magdalen put her arms around her again and said penitently, "I'm sorry, Iseult. I'm so sorry. For all of this."

They held each other a little, and then Mistress Payne drew back from her. "But I told Adam I had come to see how Sister Emma did. She's sleeping?"

"Her fever broke at dawn," Frevisse said. "She drank a little, and has slept and been awake and slept again since then."

Mistress Payne went to touch Sister Emma's forehead and feel her pulse. "She's cool enough," she agreed. "But her pulse worries me. Her blood seems to be moving sluggardly. Perhaps she should be bled."

"Perhaps," Frevisse agreed. "But I'd rather wait until this evening to decide. Rather than do it too soon?" She did not know how devoted Mistress Payne was to bleeding, or how much opposition she dared make to the suggestion.

After a moment's pause, Mistress Payne nodded agreement. "But ask for anything you need," she said, and turned back to Magdalen with what was clearly more on her mind. "Please be careful if Oliver sends to talk to you. Don't anger him more. Don't say anything you don't need to. Please."

Magdalen managed to smile. "I won't do any more than I can help. I don't want Oliver angry, truly."

Mistress Payne met her smile tremulously, wanting to be comforted, then nodded and left, closing the door behind her.

Magdalen drew a deep breath like a trembling cry and buried her face in her hands. "She may come to hate me for what I'm doing! I said what she needed to hear, but there's nothing I won't do to save Evan!"

Frevisse, more aware than ever of the tangled ruin they could be making of everyone's lives—and that it would never have gone this far without her help—could find nothing to answer. And Magdalen was neither child nor fool; she knew as well as Frevisse what could come of all this. Magdalen raised her head, and with no other word went to bring Evan into the light again.

She had just finished when the door opened. Magdalen straightened with a wordless cry, and Frevisse swung around so sharply that Bess froze in the doorway, frightened by both of them.

"It's me!" she said; then she was aware of Adam at her back and came the rest of the way into the room, shutting the door behind her.

Frevisse and Evan relaxed.

"Did you do it?" Magdalen demanded.

"Easily," Bess said. She went with Frevisse across the room to the bed so she could talk with her voice low before going on, breathless with excitement. "Old Nick wasn't at the Wheatsheaf but Cullum was."

"Cullum?" Magdalen asked.

"He's one of us," Evan said. "One of the better ones. You gave him the letter and all?"

"Yes. I told him it must reach Nicholas. He said he'd do it. He left when I left."

"Cullum can be depended on," Evan said. "He'll take it to Nicholas right enough." His hand tightened around Magdalen's. "Maybe by tonight this will be over."

"By tonight," Magdalen said, as if to make it a promise.

But Frevisse knew there was much more than Evan's escape: there was the pardon as well as her own return to the priory still to be arranged and explained. But these troubles she did not share.

Dinner came and she went down to it to hear the talk, but there was very little. Oliver, keeping to the house in expectation of the sheriff and crowner, was silent with a tension that had reached out to quell even his youngest children now. The servants, aware of their master's mood, ate quickly, to have the meal over and be away.

When Frevisse returned to Magdalen's room, Sister Emma was still deeply asleep, and Evan was drowsing, eased to it by Magdalen stroking his brow. His fever was still slight, and he woke gently a while later. Magdalen checked the wound then. There was still no sign of infection.

Now there was only the afternoon to be survived.

Chapter

19

NICHOLAS LOOKED AT the papers in his lap and then up at Cullum standing over him. "How did you come by these?"

Cullum, in the slow, definite way he gave to explanations, repeated what he had just said.

Appreciative laughter spread over Nicholas's face. "My cousin-dear is twice as smart as is good for her. So Evan's slipped into trouble at last, has he? And for a woman too." Nicholas laughed outright. "Tucked away in Payne's sister's bedroom! He'll be doing all right."

"He's hurt," Cullum said. "That's what the wench told me. And that you must needs hurry."

Nicholas looked past him to the rain runneling from the edges of the canvas. "I'd not mind another stint in Payne's parlor. Nor to see the look on his face when I tell him I want my man out of his sister's bedroom and no trouble about it because I can put him in deeper than he can put me." Nicholas grinned.

"Maybe you'd best hurry then," Cullum said. "There's hue and cry up for Evan, and it won't go well for him if he's taken."

"Hue and cry for what?"

"For the franklin's murder."

"Evan?" Nicholas found that idea amusing too. "He's been busier than I thought, wooing Payne's sister, slaughtering franklins."

"He wouldn't kill anyone," Cullum said disgustedly. "Not Evan. But he's in bad trouble. You'd best help him soon, the wench said."

Nicholas waved him away with a casual hand. "He's sweetly placed. Let's see what my loving cousin has sent."

The account roll and letter had suffered in being carried first under Bess's apron and then inside Cullum's shirt, but they had stayed dry. Nicholas was somewhat out of practice with his reading. He put the letter aside for the less thickly written and undoubtedly more interesting record of his money. As he worked his way through the first entries, written in Payne's clear hand, he chuckled, remembering one take and another as he read the list.

Cullum, impatient with standing, asked, "Shall I tell the men to ready? Are we going for Evan?"

Nicholas, intent on making out Payne's entries, jerked a hand at him. "In a while. I say when." Though maybe it would be simpler to let Evan be caught and hung for Colfoot's murder. Then there would be no hunt for anyone else. But that would deny him the pleasure of confronting Payne over the matter, and there were few pleasures sweeter than having the upper hand. Nicholas doubted he could deny himself the sport of twisting Payne to his own ends.

Cullum shrugged and went away to where most of the men had built up the fire under a canvas and were trying to roast two small pigeons for their inadequate dinner.

Intent on seeing how high his profits had grown by now, Nicholas went to the second page. As he worked his way down it, it gradually came to him that what he was reading did not agree with what Payne had been telling him. There was something wrong, and only slowly did he puzzle it out, so that not until the third time through did he realize the words said exactly what they seemed to say. That Payne had been lying to him. That Payne had been losing his money.

In a rage he did not try to control, Nicholas rose to his feet, crammed the pages into the front of his doublet, and heedless of the rain, went out yelling, "Someone bring me the horse, and bring it now!"

Sister Emma slept on. Evan drowsed and wakened through the unending afternoon with Magdalen always beside him. Occasionally they spoke together in low voices, but mostly were like Frevisse and Bess, silent in their waiting. Bess tried to sew, but it was only pretense. Frevisse sat praying as much as she could and willing Nicholas to come soon.

They heard Jack come to replace Adam on watch, and the children at play in the hall downstairs, and once the cook's voice raised in wrath at something in the kitchen. But no one came to the room itself. They were left alone, and as the afternoon went on, they sank into a kind of numb enduring, so that none of them were ready for a rush of children's feet on the stairs and a small girl's cheerful scream outside the door and Jack's laughter. Frevisse, Magdalen, and Bess all came to their feet on the instant, but no one was near enough to catch the door as small Kate flung into the room, red-faced with laughter and running. "He's after me!" she shrieked. "He's after me!"

"Kate!" Bess exclaimed, and tried to intercept her. But Kate dodged past her and into Magdalen's arms, crying "Save me!" as Magdalen stepped between her and Evan. Frevisse caught Bartholomew at the door as he charged in, and Magdalen caught Kate up and swung her around, back away toward the door. But Kate craned her head past her aunt's shoulder and exclaimed, "There's a man there!"

"No!" Magdalen cried.

"There *is*!" Kate insisted. And from Frevisse's hold,

Bartholomew yelled, without being able to see at all but glad of a new game, "The murderer! The murderer! Aunt Magdalen's caught the murderer!"

"Out!" Magdalen cried. "Get out!" All her gentleness gone, she set Kate down hard and pushed her at the doorway. "Go away!"

Confused by the anger breaking over her, Kate retreated. Frevisse grabbed her by the arm, and with Bartholomew in one hand and Kate in the other, swung them both toward the doorway and Jack coming in.

"Here!" Frevisse ordered, shoving them into his hands. "Take them out of here!"

Suddenly encumbered with two small children, Jack caught hold of them but was looking past her into the room. "They said—"

"Out!" Frevisse snapped at him.

"There's a man over there!" Kate cried excitedly. "I saw him!"

"I saw him too," Bartholomew joined in.

"You didn't!" Magdalen cried back at them. But the sob in her voice betrayed what was already lost. Jack, dragging the children backward with him out of the room, was already yelling over his shoulder for help and everyone to come.

Bess, terror-stricken, retreated to the farthest corner of the room, hands over her face as if to hide herself. Magdalen moved to shut the door, then knew the hopelessness of that and turned back to Evan. Frevisse stayed where she was, between them and whoever would come.

Sir Perys first, with Edward and Richard behind him; they must have been at their studies in the next room. "Stay back!" Frevisse warned in her most authoritative voice. There was nothing with which she could threaten them, but Sir Perys went backward a step, taking the boys with him; and then Jack, still yelling down the stairs, pushed the children toward Edward, nearest to him, and Edward took them.

Richard, neither easily threatened or charged with children, demanded, "What is it? *Is* there someone in there?"

"The murderer!" Bartholomew exclaimed, enjoying himself immensely. "He was trying to kill Aunt Magdalen and we stopped him!"

"Shut up!" Edward said fiercely, shaking him. "Shut up!"

And then everyone was there, in a rush up the stairs and from the solar. Iseult, caught in the middle of it with Katherine hanging frightened on her skirt, cried out to know what was happening, but went unheeded in the babble of her servants and the other children. Only Edward, bundling the children away into someone else's hold, kept his head. He pushed past Sir Perys and blocked the doorway, letting no one past. There he and Frevisse faced each other, with no words now, only their tense realization that neither of them could stop what was happening. In that moment, face to face with him, Frevisse saw the man that he could grow to be: controlled and strong and understanding more than he would ever say.

Then his father was there. Come behind all the rest, he shoved through them, swearing at them to stop their caterwauling. He had his sword unsheathed in his hand, and there were both anger and determination in his set face as he said at Edward's back, "Edward, stand away."

Slowly Edward obeyed, drawing his eyes from Frevisse.

"All of you stay out," Master Payne said, and moved forward. For only a moment Frevisse held her ground. But there was no point to it, no way that she could stop him. Caught in a nightmare feeling of helplessness, she drew aside and let him pass.

Evan had struggled to rise, had dragged himself up against his pillows, but had no strength for more. Magdalen knelt by him, staring defiantly across the room at her brother.

"Leave us be," she said in a low, commanding voice. "We've done no harm. Leave us alone."

"He's a murderer, Magdalen."

"He's *not*."

If it had been only a matter of will, she might have held her own against him, they were so much alike. But he had the sword, and his household at his back, and she had nothing but her love.

"Magdalen," Evan said gently, putting her away from him, his eyes fixed on her brother, reading his death there as clearly as she did. "Go. Let Dame Frevisse take you away. Don't stay for this."

Magdalen began to cry, soundlessly, the tears huge in her eyes before they slipped down her cheeks. "No," she whispered. "No."

Suddenly Master Payne came forward to the foot of the bed. His sword still directed at Evan, he stopped and groped and pulled from the shadows a long leather belt that snaked from his upheld hand to the floor as he straightened and held it aloft by the buckle.

"Not hidden well enough, man!" he said triumphantly. He swung around to the faces crowded in the doorway, Iseult and Edward first among them. "Here's proof! Here's evidence enough. Look at the end of it. That's blood there. New blood. Colfoot's blood."

Near the end of the tongue, the belt was darkly stained and crusted, plain to see.

Master Payne flung the belt down, out of his way, and turned on Evan. "Can't you even stand up, you coward? Hiding in my sister's bed and behind her skirts. You deserve to die for that alone!"

"He's hurt!" Magdalen cried, trying to put herself between Evan and her brother.

But Evan held her away, and begged in desperation, "Dame Frevisse, take her out of here!"

Frevisse moved, but there was no time. Master Payne was already around the bed, his arm drawn back for the thrust that Evan could not avoid.

"Payne!"

The roar from the doorway brought Payne around on his heel, instinctively crouched to face a new threat.

Nicholas shoved past Edward into the room. "Payne, you lying dog! Where's my fortune?" He dragged the crumpled account pages from the front of his tunic and threw them on the floor. "You've done nothing but lose my money! I'm no better off than when I started!"

"Nicholas, that isn't—" Frevisse began.

But Payne, dark-faced with new anger, cut across her words. "You're right! You were a cur when you started and you're a cur now!"

"You lying cheat!" Nicholas yelled, drawing his sword and closing on him. "I want my fortune! And if I can't have it, I'll have your blood instead!"

Payne brought up his own sword between them. All the hatred for each other that they had buried for the sake of mutual gain was now in the naked open.

"Nicholas, your pardon!" Frevisse cried. "Listen to me!"

Unheeding, Nicholas thrust at Payne. Payne caught it aside with his own blade, more ready than Nicholas had expected. Mistress Payne screamed, and would have thrown herself between them, but Edward caught her by the arm and waist and held her back. "No, Mother!"

Frevisse backed into the narrow space between Evan's bed and the wall, trapping Magdalen behind her.

The room was too small for wide swordplay. Payne and Nicholas could only manage thrust and slice, their swords held double-handed in front of them for shield and weapon both. Neither was much skilled, and both were plainly long out of practice. But Payne's skill had come in the casual way of needing protection in his travels, while Nicholas in his long-since youth had at least had proper training. It showed as he knocked aside Payne's heavy thrusts, not able to force in any of his own but better able to defend himself.

They went clumsily, in ragged starts and stops, a little down the room, then back to its center. Stunned, no one interfered. Even Mistress Payne made no more outcry, but stood huddled against Edward, her fists clenched to her mouth.

Then Nicholas's sword caught along Payne's blade. Nicholas wrenched his sword around, and Payne's sword broke loose from his hands and clattered wide away from him across the floor. Payne jerked backward, head up, still angry but his hands spread out, surrendering. Nicholas without even pause lunged forward, driving his blade in to the left of and under Payne's breastbone. Then he jerked back, hauling it out, and blood followed, gouting down the front of Payne's gown. Payne reached to stop it but was already falling. And dead before he reached the floor.

Chapter
⚜ **20** ⚜

NICHOLAS STEPPED BACK, panting heavily. With a gesture of finish and satisfaction, he let the blade's point drop toward the floor, and was not ready for Edward's anguished cry and single forward movement that scooped his father's sword from the floor at his feet and brought it up, then around and down as he leaped at Nicholas. Nicholas barely jerked his own sword up in time to catch the blow, but the force of it drove him backward and Edward so headlong after him that they grappled together.

Iseult, in the doorway, turned wildly on the men behind her and screamed, "Stop them!"

Released from their shock, Adam, Jack, and Tam pushed forward into the room. Before Nicholas could break free from Edward, they were on them, Tam pulling Edward away, Jack and Adam grabbing Nicholas from behind, twisting his sword from his hand and wrenching his arms up behind his back.

Nicholas fought, but they had him. They forced him first to his knees, then jerked him to his feet as Edward ordered, "Take him out of here. Put him in the barn. Tie him and guard him."

"You dog's whelp!" Nicholas raged. "I'll kill you next and anyone else between me and mine!"

"Take him out!" Edward yelled.

They did; and by the way his shouting cut off suddenly on the stairs, someone knocked him senseless on the way.

By then Mistress Payne was kneeling beside her husband, bent over and weeping on his back. Richard, crying too, was trying to put his arms around her. The three younger children, not fully understanding yet what they had only half seen, stood staring around Sir Perys and the maidservants in the doorway.

"Take them away," Frevisse said quietly to anyone who would; and the two women did, gently drawing the children back, herding them away to somewhere else.

Behind her Magdalen had crumpled down beside Evan, clinging to him, her face hidden in his shoulder while he held her as close as he could.

Edward stood where Tam had left him in the middle of the room, dry-eyed, staring down at his father's body, his hands held out open and empty at his sides.

The only sounds in the room were Iseult's and Richard's crying, and Sir Perys's hurried prayers from the doorway.

Then Jack and Adam returned. Frevisse stirred from her own paralysis, knowing things had to be done. As they hesitated behind Sir Perys, she said quietly, "You had best move Master Payne's body to his own bed. Bess, help Mistress Payne."

At a direct order, Bess was able to move, to come forward from her corner and draw Mistress Payne to her feet with Richard's help so the men could lift her husband's body carefully between them and carry it out of the room. Bess, Mistress Payne, Richard, and Sir Perys followed after them.

Edward stayed where he was, did not even lift his head to watch their going. Behind him, Frevisse picked up the forgotten belt, rolled it, and holding it, tucked her hands up her sleeves.

"Edward," she said.

He looked around at her, slowly, as if uncertain he was still able to move and see. She went to stand in front of him.

"Edward, the sheriff and crowner will be here, probably soon."

Edward tried to answer, but no words came; he was still too empty with shock.

"Would you have me speak to them first?" she offered. "To explain what's happened?"

Vaguely, trying to draw his mind around to it, he said, "I have to talk to them. I should—"

Frevisse gripped his arm to make him look at her. "No. You should not." Holding his eyes with her own, she said very slowly and forcefully, "Edward, listen to me. You know Evan did not kill Colfoot."

Edward tensed and made as if to draw away from her hand. Then he steadied, and as if finally fully conscious of her said in a rather desperate voice, "I know."

"Because you know your father did it."

Edward opened his mouth, protest in every line of his body. Frevisse dug her fingers more deeply into his arm and repeated ruthlessly, "You know your father did it. No peddler ever wore a belt like the one your father showed us. That's a rich man's belt. Your father brought it deliberately into the room to accuse Evan of the murder. But it was your father who killed Colfoot."

Edward began to shake his head in denial. Again Frevisse cut him off, driving her words at him. "Edward, your father is dead. He can't be hurt by our saying this. No accusation can touch him anymore. Do you truly think he would want it otherwise, now that he's dead?"

Edward shuddered and dragged his eyes away from her. "No. He wouldn't."

"Then that is what I will tell the sheriff and the crowner when they come. That your father went out after Colfoot in a rage and killed him. You didn't even know about it until now. They won't have many questions for you after that. Do you understand?"

His whole body stiff with pain, Edward nodded.

In the bed Sister Emma stirred; she would shortly be awake. Frevisse, aware of how much simpler few questions would be—and that Edward needed to do something more than stand imprisoned with his thoughts—said to him, "Evan should not be here when Sister Emma awakes. A man in her room would sorely distress her. Will you help Magdalen move him to your bed?"

Edward, ready now to do what he was told, nodded again. Together he and Magdalen helped Evan to his feet and, with most of his weight on Edward, took him out of the room.

Sister Emma roused with heavy coughing. It jerked her fully awake, and before Frevisse could give her anything to drink, she had sat up and leaned over the side of bed, beginning to throw up.

Frevisse caught up a basin from the table and held it for her until she had finished, then helped her ease back on the pillows and wiped her face with a damp cloth.

"I feel awful," Sister Emma moaned. "Awful."

"You'll feel better soon, now that that's out of you," Frevisse said. She hoped she was right, but Sister Emma's pallor was alarming.

Bess had returned and been waiting. Now she came forward, and after she had felt Sister Emma's face and laid an ear against her chest to listen to her breathing, she said, "Her fever hasn't come back and the rheum's not sunk into her lungs. It's the medicine in her now that's making her feel worse. She'll be better for being awake and sitting up."

"And eating something," Sister Emma croaked. "I think I'm starving."

Frevisse and Bess exchanged looks. "She'll mend," Bess said, and went to see what could be found in the kitchen.

Frevisse stayed with Sister Emma, and when Bess returned with broth and bread and ale, took the duty of feeding her while Bess, without a word, went with a cloth to clean the blood from the floor where Master Payne had fallen. Sister Emma could not see it from where she lay; Frevisse kept her own face turned away, unable to watch.

When they were both done, Frevisse gave Sister Emma's care over to Bess and left without explanation. As she had told Edward, the sheriff and crowner would be there, probably soon, and there were matters she had to see to before they arrived.

She went to Magdalen and Evan first. They were alone in Edward and Richard's room. Magdalen had been weeping, but was quiet now. Evan was as white and sunken with exhaustion as Frevisse felt. Neither of them said anything as Frevisse entered. She was not sure whether their silence was because there was nothing else to say, or because there was too much. Through the wall, unintelligible, she could hear Sister Emma's unwitting chatter.

"You heard what I said to Edward?" Frevisse asked. "About Colfoot?"

"That Oliver killed him," Magdalen said brokenly. "Did he?"

"How else did he come by that bloodied belt that both you and I know was never Evan's? Why else would he want so badly to have Evan be the murderer if not to cover his own guilt?"

"And you're going to tell the sheriff?" Evan asked.

"I'm going to tell him that, and about the quarrel Oliver had with Colfoot and Colfoot's threats that drove Oliver to kill him."

"What will you say about Evan?" Magdalen asked.

"That he's a peddler and your lover and that Oliver meant to use him as scapegoat for Colfoot's murder."

"And when Nicholas tells him I'm one of his men?" Evan asked.

"I have things to say to Nicholas that will keep him quiet on that point," Frevisse said grimly. "And if he isn't, then we'll deny and deny and deny it again. We'll say we sent the accounts to him with promise of reward if he used them to make Master Payne let you go unharmed. We were desperate and that seemed the only hope. I'll tell the sheriff that, and you will tell him that, and that is all that we will tell him. Our word will weigh far more than Nicholas's, in any event. And if we don't convince him, I have other recourse. There's still the matter of the pardons I asked my uncle for."

"You'll still seek pardon for Nicholas?" Evan asked.

"No." There was no urge to good in Nicholas after all; apart from everything else, he had killed Oliver Payne in plain murder after Payne had surrendered. "There'll be no pardon for Nicholas. But you and the others, I think, will have yours. I'll plead to my uncle for them."

Magdalen began to cry openly. Frevisse left Evan holding her, and went down to face the one person she wanted to face even less than the sheriff and crowner.

Nicholas was tied by the waist to one of the posts in the center of the barn. Another rope had been thrown up over a beam and his arms tied above his head so that he stood at full height, unable to sit or even slump. Blood had run down his neck from a cut above his ear and there was a darkening bruise below one eye. His eyes were closed, but Frevisse thought he was aware.

The barn was shadowy, warm with cattle smells and straw. Tam the stableman rose from his seat on an overturned bucket as she entered. A dagger was laid conspicuously on the straw beside him, but he had a piece of harness in his hands as if he had been mending it. "M'lady?"

"I want to talk to him," Frevisse said. Tam looked doubtfully at Nicholas, whose eyes had opened and were now fixed on her. "He's sinned," she said. "I want to help him pray."

"Ah. Right." Tam could see the sense in that. "Go on then."

"Could you . . ." She gestured farther along the barn. "So he can pray more freely? Just a little farther off. Not out of sight."

Tam could see the sense in that too, picked up his dagger, and went perhaps fifteen feet further away. Frevisse went close to Nicholas.

"I hope you have a dagger up one of your sleeves, cousin," he said. "This is damnably uncomfortable and I want out of here."

"No dagger, Nicholas. No escape."

"Then you're not much use!" he snarled. "And I don't want your damned prayers. Leave, damn you!"

"The sheriff and the crowner will be here soon. We must talk."

Wary hope rose in his face. "You have a plan? The pardon maybe?"

"The pardon is in my uncle's control. What you have to do is keep silent about Evan."

"Evan? Why should he go free while I don't? I'll say anything I can and he can hang right next to me if it comes to that."

"Evan hasn't killed a man in front of witnesses," Frevisse said between her teeth.

"He asked for it!" Nicholas retorted. "It was a fair fight; he had a sword!"

"Keep your voice down. Leave Evan out of this and people will go on thinking he's only a peddler and only ask him the questions they'd ask a peddler. But if you say he's one of your men, there'll be different questions, ones he'll answer to save his own skin. Do you want Evan telling everything he knows about you? Telling every tale he has of what you've done?"

Nicholas glared around the barn as if seeking for a better

answer than the one she was demanding from him, but there was none. Refusing to look at her, he said, "I'll leave Evan out of it."

"Magdalen and I will say we sent you the accounts with evidence of Master Payne's cheating because we wanted your help in taking her lover out of her brother's house. We promised you a reward. That's what we'll say and that's what you'd better say."

"He did worse than cheat me. The damn fool lost my money!"

"He hadn't lost your money. If you'd bothered to read the letter that came with the accounts or used your eyes half as well as you use your mouth, you'd know the second page was all false. In fear you'd be pardoned and come demanding your profits, Payne rewrote it so you'd think you had hardly more than you'd started with. He was cheating you but the money was still there!" Frevisse lost control of her voice. It rose with anger and pain and her own shame for her part in all of it. "We gave you the evidence to demand it from him, only you killed him instead!"

Not able to stomach him anymore, or her broken hopes of his redemption, she turned her back on him and left.

Lovie met her in the screens passage, flustered and anxious. "My lady, they've come! They're just riding into the yard. The sheriff and crowner and all their men! What do we do?"

"We have them brought into the hall, and tell Mistress Payne and Master Edward they've come and that I'll speak to them as Master Edward and I agreed."

"Will you?" Lovie sounded awed. "All by yourself?"

"All by myself," Frevisse said wearily. What she truly wanted was to be entirely alone, to deny that any of the past four days had happened. But it was not finished yet. Not until she had spoken to these men who would ask questions she did not want to answer. Not until she had made them believe the mix of lies and truths she was going to tell them.

She waited for them in the hall, composing herself outwardly far more than she could inwardly. They came, with Lovie hasty at their side to introduce them. To Frevisse's relief she knew neither of them. If the crowner had been Master Montfort from her own side of Oxfordshire, he might have tried to find other answers than the ones she gave him, merely out of his deep dislike for her that had grown from their other encounters. But this crowner was an older man, with a settled countenance, who would listen to a responsible description of the facts, and build his conclusion from that.

The sheriff was younger, with a keen eye, and said as they were introduced and Frevisse curtseyed to them both, "Master Payne is indeed dead?"

The distance between door and hall had been time enough for Lovie to tell at least that much.

"Yes," Frevisse said, forcing her voice to steadiness. "He was killed in front of all of us. We have the man who did it tied up in the barn."

"Is it the peddler? The one Payne had the hunt up for, for killing Colfoot?" the sheriff asked.

"No. The peddler didn't kill Colfoot." Her hands tucked up her habit's sleeves tightened painfully on her forearms, but she still held her voice even. "Master Payne killed Colfoot. Master Payne was killed by an outlaw he had had dealings with. That's who we have prisoner in the barn."

She had been too intent on the sheriff and crowner to more than marginally notice the half dozen of their men who had come in with them. Now a familiar voice said, "Frevisse? You mean Nicholas?"

Hardly daring to believe, caught between relief and alarm, she saw past the sheriff and crowner to Thomas Chaucer coming toward her. Elegant in blue riding houppelande, furred hat, and high boots, he had his usual way of

looking as if he belonged where he was and expected to be
obeyed in anything he said. Though he had consistently
through the years refused the honors of nobility offered to
him by the Crown he served, he had wealth and power
enough that he lacked no authority he cared to assert. And
he was the dearest friend she had.

Now, clearly known to the sheriff and crowner, he held
out his hand to her, and she gratefully took it as he said by
way of introduction, "This is my niece I told you of. Is it
Nicholas you have in the barn?"

Frevisse nodded.

Chaucer forbore to say the several things she saw cross
his mind. Instead he said, "I have someone else you may be
glad of too," and gestured behind him to Master Naylor
come from among the other men.

Relief as great as the fear she had secretly carried since
the outlaws had taken him from the camp suffused her. "Oh,
I am glad you're all right!" Frevisse exclaimed. "I wasn't
sure . . ."

"I'm well," he said, bowing to her.

"But I think all that needs to be told should be told
somewhere more private than this," Chaucer said. "And
hopefully in comfort. Geoff? James? You agree?"

The sheriff nodded. "It sounds as if there's a deal of
telling," he agreed.

"This is too fine a house to lack a solar," Chaucer
suggested. "Or is there a parlor? And something to drink
perhaps."

She took them to the parlor and, careful of everything she
said, told them all that needed to be told to make as much
of an end as there could be to everything that had happened.

Pale, watery sunshine fell weakly yellow through the
window and across the floor of the parlor. While she talked,
Frevisse watched the shadow of a joint stool move slowly
across the carpet, because the shadow had nothing to do

with anything that mattered. It had no passion of love or hate or greed or any other thing. And that lack was very comforting just now.

She talked, and the men listened; and when she had finished, the sheriff and crowner thanked him for making it all clear and simple, and then went to question others in the household and Nicholas.

Exhausted, still staring at the shadow of the stool, Frevisse slumped down in her chair. She doubted they would learn aught that would hurt her tale. She wished there had been no need to say any of it.

Quietly, evenly, Chaucer said, "That was well done, Frevisse. Now suppose you tell me the part you didn't tell them."

Frevisse let out a deep and trembling breath. "Was it that plain?"

"Not to anyone who doesn't know you well. What else happened?"

She cast a look at Master Naylor standing quietly out of the way in a corner. His face was lined with tiredness and the strain of a man who had not rested in several days. Avoiding her uncle's question, she said, "Master Naylor, I need to ask your pardon for siding against you in the outlaws' camp."

The steward was rarely given to smiling, but his eyes held a shadowy amusement. "Hasting me away from there before I forced Nicholas out of patience, you likely saved me from what came to Master Payne."

"You also loosed him to come to me," Thomas put in.

"Not back to Domina Edith?" Frevisse asked.

"To Domina Edith first after Sister Emma's family," Master Naylor assured her. "And she sent me on to Master Chaucer, in time to reach him when your letter from here did."

"Did you send her word of that?" Frevisse asked, with

memory of the letter she had never written to her prioress.

"Of that, and that we were going to fetch you home," Chaucer said. "Her mind is as at ease as it can be until you ride back through the priory gates. Now, what is it you haven't told us?"

Chaucer was not a man to be balked, whether in Parliament or in private. Carefully, Frevisse explained that Evan was not merely a peddler, that he was one of Nicholas's outlaws; and described, in greater detail than she had given the sheriff and crowner, her help to Magdalen in saving and hiding him. Only at the last, when she added her guilt in deliberately drugging Sister Emma, did she bow her head, letting her shame show. She had known at the time what she was doing, and been willing to take the burden of it, but it sounded worse told aloud to others than it had in her own mind while she did it. Almost everything she had done these past few days sounded worse told aloud and at length. Abuse of Sister Emma's trust was only one of her sins. She had lied repeatedly. Betrayed the people who had given her shelter. Helped bring about Master Payne's death. Deceived apparently without end.

"It's done, Frevisse," Chaucer said. He laid a hand on her arm.

Her hands, out of sight up her sleeves, tightened. It was penance she was in need of now, not sympathy. Wearily she pointed out, "Because of what I did, Nicholas is a prisoner, guilty of murder, and a man is dead who would not be if I'd not interfered."

"You couldn't see what would come of what you did."

"I might have seen if I'd looked. But I didn't look. And outcome or not, what I did were sins. And behind them all was the worst sin. Pride. My pride that made me believe that I should interfere because I knew best what should be done."

"Only pride, Frevisse?" Chaucer's doubt was warm with

sympathy. "Not affection? Not desire to help those in direct need, who had no other help but you to turn to? Only pride?"

"I don't know," she whispered. "I can't judge now. I don't know."

Chaucer released her. They knew each other's minds well; in a different situation they could have cheerfully argued the matter far into the night, but there was no cheer in her just now. Instead, he responded to the strain behind her voice. "Do you wish to leave here now? As soon as may be? I know someone who lives not far from here where you could go instead."

Frevisse very desperately wanted to be away, but without raising her head she answered, "Sister Emma can't travel today. Her cough is still heavy. Tomorrow."

"Tomorrow then. Or longer if need be. We'll stay here until she can travel."

"Will the crowner allow it before he's finished investigating?" Master Naylor asked.

"I don't see why not," Chaucer said. "Frevisse has told him all she can tell him. And if I can't persuade James of that, I can give recognizance for her, that she won't go anywhere he can't find her. I think my word will stretch that far." He smiled. "Is there anything I can do for you at present, Frevisse?"

She shook her head. "Just be here. It helps to know you are." To know that if she could not carry this through, she could turn to him for help. "I had better go see how Sister Emma fares."

She found Mistress Payne and her children—Katherine, Kate, and Bartholomew ranged on one side of her, Richard on the other—praying beside her husband's body in the great bedroom. They were not yet dressed in mourning, but were all kneeling with their heads bowed, silent except for an occasional shivery sob from one of the little girls.

Magdalen was there too, but on the far side of the bed from them, deep in her own prayers for her brother's soul. Sir Perys read prayers for the dead at the foot of the bed, and Lovie and Maud stood at hand to help if anything were needed.

Only Edward was missing. But he was Master Edward now, head of the family, and probably with the sheriff and crowner. The adulthood he had been assuming a few days ago was fully and too soon come on him.

Lastly Frevisse made herself look at Oliver Payne laid out on the bed. His wife and her women had already cleaned his body and dressed him in the red houppelande he had worn when Frevisse first met him. In death his face had the reposed confidence of that evening. She gazed on it a long while, unable to break the brittle, grieving peace of the scene, not wanting to do what she had to do next.

But necessity was stronger than desire. With a brief prayer, she crossed herself and went to lay a hand on Mistress Payne's shoulder.

She looked up, and Frevisse saw that she was between tears just now. The first shock of grief had passed; long and deep-set grieving had not yet taken hold. In that pause between the onrush and floods of sorrow, she was dazed but not blind with pain. And she had no knowledge yet of what part Frevisse had had in her husband's dying.

So her look was only questioning. And when Frevisse moved her head to show she wanted her to come away, she paused to murmur one more prayer, crossed herself, and came.

Frevisse had been unable to think of anywhere to go that would be both private and not excite questions from anyone who saw them. So they went simply to the head of the stairs between the Paynes' room and Magdalen's, where no one could overhear or come to them unknown.

Briefly Frevisse explained that her uncle had come and

that she and Sister Emma would be leaving as soon as possible, probably on the morrow, to ease the family's burden at least a little. Mistress Payne made no answer beyond a nod. Words, like tears, were temporarily drained out of her. She was so small a woman, and so drawn in around her grief, that she seemed hardly more than a child now, standing in front of Frevisse with her head drooping, her face hidden.

But Frevisse went on. "I've spoken to Edward. Has he told you of that? Of what we agreed to tell the sheriff? That it wasn't Magdalen's Evan who killed Colfoot. That it was your husband."

Mistress Payne shivered. And still did not look up. But nodded.

Frevisse brought her right hand out of her left sleeve where she had kept it all this while, and held out the bloodied belt she had caught up from Magdalen's floor. Mistress Payne's head jerked sharply away from it. "The sheriff will want you to say this was your husband's. Will you do that?" Frevisse asked.

Mistress Payne's head jerked again, caught between nod and denial. But she said, her voice cracking with grief, "He's dead. I'll say it. It won't hurt him now."

"But you know it isn't his. Don't you?"

Mistress Payne's head finally came up. Her eyes widened on Frevisse's face but she said nothing.

Gently, very gently, Frevisse said, "It's Edward's, isn't it?"

"No." The strength that Magdalen had said was in her sister-in-law now showed itself. "No. It's my husband's. I've told you so. I'll tell the sheriff and crowner so if they ask me. It's my husband's belt."

"The wear mark on the buckle in the leather," Frevisse said, holding it out so she could see, "shows it went around a waist much narrower than your husband's. A boy's waist. Edward's."

Mistress Payne seized the belt out of her hands. In rapid, jerking movements, she coiled it up buckle inward, covering the mark, leaving the bloodied end to hang free. "It was my husband's belt," she repeated.

"That's what you must keep saying." Frevisse assured her. "But I want to know how Edward came to fight with Colfoot. He's told you about it?"

Mistress Payne held silent a moment longer, but perhaps it was a relief to say what would never be said to anyone else. A relief to say what she had thought would have to stay sealed in her forever. Or perhaps she simply bent to what she could not avoid. "He heard the quarrel between his father and Colfoot, and Colfoot's threats against both us and Magdalen. When Colfoot left here, Edward went after him, not even taking a horse. He just cut through the woods and intercepted him along the road. Edward didn't mean anything, only to talk with him, to try to talk him out of it. But Colfoot was still in a fury. He saw Edward as no more than an intruding child, and cursed at him and brought out his sword and struck him over the shoulders with the flat of it. Edward lost his temper. He had only his dagger, but they were so close together and Colfoot wasn't expecting it, and I think Edward killed him before either of them knew what they were doing. He didn't believe he'd done it, only that somehow he'd pulled Colfoot from his horse. But when he knelt by him, Colfoot was almost dead, and died while Edward was looking at him. Then Edward was frightened. He cleaned the dagger in the grass and came home. He was so frightened. He didn't know he had bloodied his belt. I saw it when he came in. It had to be by God's mercy I was the first to see him when he came home. He looked so torn and in pain. We didn't know what to do. I couldn't let anyone else see him. And I had to do something about the belt, but I didn't know what. So we went to his father, in the parlor where no one would come if Oliver didn't let them. It seemed the only safe place. We were all so frightened."

Her voice trailed away, remembering not only her fear but her husband's, for Edward.

Gently Frevisse said, "Then your husband hid the belt until he could have a chance to be safely rid of it?" Mistress Payne nodded dumbly. "And Edward put on different clothes so its lack would not be so apparent. And at supper that night Master Payne had the idea of making the stranger in the orchard out to be the murderer."

Mistress Payne sighed. "It seemed the safest, the simplest thing to do. We didn't know he was Magdalen's lover."

"And when you did, it didn't matter, because he was still no more than a peddler and no one but Magdalen would care if he died."

"It was . . . necessary," Mistress Payne agreed softly. She moved past remembering to what was necessary now. "Are you going to let us keep our secret?"

Lying. Deception. Abuse of trust. Here they all were, joined together in a single act. For this more than all the rest, there would be penance so deep in her own heart that she might never be free of it. But the choice had been made already.

Quietly Frevisse said, "I've helped you make it. I'll help you keep it. Tell Edward that he'll have my daily prayers through all his life to come."

INTRODUCING...
Exciting New Mysteries Every Month